So as Not to Die Alone

by

Lisa Johnson Mitchell

Finishing Line Press
Georgetown, Kentucky

So as Not to Die Alone

ACKNOWLEDGMENTS

Many thanks to Bennington Writing Seminars and my beloved mentors, Dallas Writing Workshops and my incredible teachers, and lastly, my precious family for all their love and support.

Publisher: Leah Huete de Maines
Editor: Christen Kincaid
Cover Art: Photo by Lisa Johnson Mitchell
Author Photo: Hal Samples
Cover Design: James Laurence Mitchell

Order online: www.finishinglinepress.com
also available on amazon.com

Author inquiries and mail orders:
Finishing Line Press
PO Box 1626
Georgetown, Kentucky 40324
USA

Contents

"Wonderland"

I'd been working on logos for my client, Fondueligans, for five hours and if I had to do one more, I was going to scream. But I was the lead graphic designer on the account, so I had no choice. When the marketing gurus decided on the restaurant's name, I pointed out that Fondueligans was an odd mash-up of Irish (Hooligan) and French (Fondue). "You're being too literal," my boss said. "It's catchy."

Fondueligans' signature dish was the "The Hooligan Fondueligan"—an epicurean extravaganza that featured an assortment of sausages, cheeses, and fruit (mostly melons) that you dipped into various vein-clogging sauces with long, cloven-hoofed tongs. They were served to customers by "hooligans" played by actors who were studying theater at the local community college.

Sal, the Fondueligans' Creative Director and my boss, was a tyrannical Italian who kept asking me to change the font size—make it bigger, then smaller—then he told me to go back to where I started. After I presented what I thought were brilliant designs, he demanded that I switch the typeface from the always-tasteful Times New Roman to Log Cabin, then to Groovy Chick. He finally settled on Porcupine Pickle.

It was almost 6 p.m. and the cleaning service was making a ruckus with the vacuum, so it was hard for me to concentrate. I decided to stop what I was doing—I'd finished everything for my 8 a.m. presentation and besides, I had a date to meet Glenn, this guy I'd connected with on a dating site I was trying, Great Expectations. Despite the site's Dickensian name, one of my friends had met her husband this way. I wasn't looking for a guy with lots of money who wore designer suits and expensive shoes. But I sure didn't want a guy with a bad haircut who still lived with his parents. I dreamed of someone normal. Normal with an artistic flair would be nice.

I was done with blind dates. The last guy I'd been set up with came to my door wearing an Easter bunny tie (it wasn't even Easter), shorts, and slip-on tennis shoes without the backs. When I saw him, I almost said, "Jan isn't here. I'm her roommate."

A few days ago, I discovered Glenn when I snuck online during lunch. I was eating my fat-free, taste-free frozen dinner: Rancho Enchiladas with a whisper of peas. Most guys on the site were electricians, in IT, or sales. When I read that he was a designer, I immediately sent him an email. On his profile, he claimed to be about six feet tall (good because I was 5'11"), had salt and pepper hair (looked a little older like me), and dark eyes. No double chin. Appeared to have all his teeth.

Glenn and I decided to meet at Fondueligans. It was close by and I had a coupon I could use, one I designed, but of course, Sal had to go and mess that up, too. He forced me to use the headline, "We put the U in FondUeligans—50% off for U." I thought bringing the coupon on our date was a nice gesture to help Glenn save a little money. Graphic designers are notoriously underpaid. (I should know.) I wasn't crazy about eating fondue. Not only because I had to think about it all day at work, but also because I was not very coordinated. I didn't trust myself with those sharp pointy tongs along with the terribly hot cheese.

Though the interior at Fondueligans was brand new, it still felt like classic 1970s: fake wood paneling, along with gold, green, and orange cushions on the chairs. Weird smells that I couldn't put my finger on. Across the back wall was a mural of the Swiss Alps, the area in France where fondue originated. Posters of the Eiffel Tower, the Arc de Triomphe, and bucolic French country sides adorned the hallway to the restrooms. On the tables sat frosted lamps, a nod to Paris Metro designer Hector Guimard. When I took a seat at the bar, the heel of my new platform pumps got hung up on the stool's leg. I pulled out my compact and examined my face: my eyes were not too made up and my lips were a soft, pinky red, a new shade I had bought at the suggestion of a chatty, boundary-free sales lady at Macy's.

The minute Glenn walked in, I knew it was him. He actually looked like his picture. I waved a faint, awkward "hello." When he saw me, he hurried over. He had on jeans, a button-down shirt, and non-descript, possibly orthopedic black lace-up shoes. We shook hands, then gave each other concave chest hugs. He brushed the salt-and-pepper hair away from his saucery brown eyes. He had a few wrinkles on his forehead. His teeth were all there—gleaming.

"Hello Princess, so glad to make your acquaintance." He kissed my hand.

"Hello, to you, too…Mr. Prince." I had no idea why I said that. We settled into our black leather barstools. The music, a medley of French torch songs, was not too loud; we could hear ourselves talk.

"I just love fondue. It's so fonDOable," Glenn said.

"That's funny!" I said, way too enthusiastically. "I work on the account, so I get my daily fill."

"Must get old." Glenn started flipping through the menu, swatting the pages with his fingertips. He was wearing a thick, gold ring with a dark, red stone on his middle finger.

"So how 'bout it? Shall we get some fondue? Quiche? There's so many kinds of cheeses," he said. He bent close to the menu, squinting like he was trying to decode the mysteries of an ancient scroll.

"That'll work," I lied. I was on Weight Watchers. The onslaught of cheese and meat would set me back a bit with my diet, but I was wearing a new black dress I had just been able to squeeze into after three years. I didn't feel like a walrus any more.

"Actually, I'd like a salad," Glenn said.

That's kind of cute, wanting a salad. He's not afraid to show his feminine side.

"What is this?" Glenn said. "Knee…knee-coyse salad?"

"Niçoise. Nee-swa. It means a person who is from Nice, France."

"Well ooh la la!" He closed the menu, then smoothed it with his fingers.

"There are some Irish beers." I pointed to the list. "A lame attempt by marketing to merge the themes of Irish and French. I mean, who drinks beer with fondue? Wine is best."

"I wouldn't know any different."

"The whole concept of this place is disturbing."

The waiter, our hooligan, appeared. He had a decent build and was wearing a white t-shirt that hugged his pot belly, jeans, combat boots—and a scowl. His eyes were dead and bloodshot. "Doug" was on his nametag.

"Welcome to Fondueligans. Take your order," he snarled. "What are we drinking tonight?" When people spoke to me in plurals, I felt obliged to return the pronoun.

"We'll have a merlot."

"And you," Doug stated, as if an accusation.

"I'll have a mimosa."

Doug's face was stiff as if he was paralyzed. "Merci," he said, then clomped away.

"Gracias!" Glenn called.

"Good one," I said. "What languages do you speak?"

"Only the language of love—KIDDING," Glenn said. "Just a bit of Spanish. You?

"Un poco de Espanol and a smidge of French." I zeroed in on Glenn's bulbous ring and as mean thoughts started popping up, I heard my grandmother's voice. You're just too "ticky," a word she used for "particular." No doubt my ticky-ness was the reason for my decades of bitter loneliness.

Doug returned with Glenn's mimosa and my red wine. The glasses thumped on the faux-wood bar.

"What do you want," Doug announced.

"I'll have the, uh," Glenn said, pointing to the menu, "NEE-SWA salad."

"And we'll share the Hooligan Fondueligan. Here's a coupon for 50% off," I said.

"Yep," Doug said. He lumbered away.

Glenn swiveled his barstool towards me and his knee bumped my thigh.

"Oh, excuse me."

"No problem—sorry, didn't mean to say 'no problem'—that saying gets on my nerves. It seems to have replaced 'you're welcome,' you know, when you say, 'thank you' and the response is 'no problem.' I hear it all the time from the 20-somethings and I want to say, 'I wasn't thinking about any problems until *you brought them up.*'"

"Well put." Our eyes met. We had a connection, which eclipsed my disdain for his man jewelry.

We segued into interview mode: Where were you born? Where do you like to vacation? What's your opinion of hot tubs?

I learned Glenn was from Oklahoma and he learned I was afraid of clowns. He collected Civil War memorabilia and I collected thimbles. He was a Summer and I was an Autumn.

Doug emerged from behind the kitchen's saloon doors and placed Glenn's salad and the fondue in front of us. The steam rose from the cheese. His face was sweating as he handed us our utensils.

"I am terrible with this whole thing," I said, moving my tong in a wide circle around the fondue pot. "So daunt—"

Doug interrupted. "Listen up, you got sausages here. Over here, cheddar, Swiss, some Gouda; then over here are your fruits."

Doug retreated into the kitchen.

"You should go first," I said. "I insist."

Glenn impaled a few meats and cheese with his pointy utensil, plunged it into the cauldron of yellow, and popped them in his mouth. His eyes started to water and he pulled out a blue silk handkerchief and dabbed his eyes.

"Whoa! That's hot, but delicious," he said, through a mouthful of mush.

I grasped my weapon and stuck it into a few sausage rounds, sunk them into the vat, and took a bite. The fires of hell rained down on my tongue; a blinding shock of heat ran from my crown to my toes. I jerked my torso up so straight I was sure the curvature in my spine was instantly corrected. I spit what was in my mouth out onto my palm.

"Ooouch!"

Glenn immediately handed me his hanky. I wiped my face, then chugged my wine.

"Water!" I gasped for air. "More drinks!"

Doug emerged from behind the kitchen's saloon doors. I was sure he was high.

"Water, please! And another round," Glenn said. He rubbed my back as I cradled my mouth in my hands.

"Okay," Doug said, moving in slow motion, as if he was encased in syrup.

"Gosh, I'm so sorry," Glenn said. He patted me on the back; his fingers pressed on my spinal cord.

Doug reappeared and plunked the drinks on the counter. I downed the wine, then the water, both of which did little to soothe my aching, swollen tongue.

My mother was an alcoholic, so I didn't really drink very much. I had a low tolerance for liquor and was attempting to pace myself.

After a few more drinks, I was alternating between water and wine. My tongue was better, but the room was starting to tilt. The bottles behind the bar blurred and the light bounced off them, crashing into my eyes. I tried to talk but I couldn't control my lips. I was not sure what I was saying. My mouth felt like it was full of gravel.

Finally, I pushed out a wad of words. "Sooo what do you design? Haaaave...haaaave you seeeen....my purse?"

"It's right here on the hook." Glenn lifted my designer purse, my 40th birthday present to myself, from a hook beneath the bar and displayed it for me. "Listen, why don't we go to my place for some coffee? I have this Turkish blend that'll knock your socks off."

Socks sounded good. Right then, I wished I could have climbed into a giant tube sock and fallen asleep.

"Oh, but you can't drive," Glenn said.

"Let's take a cab," I slurred.

"Okay," Glenn said. "No, what about this: I'll drive us in *your* car to *my* place and leave my car here. Then you can drive *me* back down here when you're able. Check please, Doug?"

I woke up. I was nestled into a deep purple couch adorned with a fuss of colorful pillows in Glenn's peanut-sized apartment. The carpet was beige shag. On the walls were photos of sunsets across an ocean. A few lithographs with Arabic inscriptions. And a headshot of a woman wearing a burka. Her eyes were mysterious and seemed to follow me around the room. The lights were off except for one small, gold lamp that cast a spotlight on the wall. Candles were burning. On the ceiling were large, paisley scarves meant to suggest a sultan's den.

I sipped on bitter, mud-like coffee in a clear glass cup and saucer; the steam bathed my cheeks. Glenn had changed into grey jogging pants and was sitting cross-legged on the floor. Exotic music was playing. A woman with a shaky voice was singing. Occasionally there was a Muslim call to prayer mixed into the electronic music that accompanied her mournful solo. It appeared I had travelled from Fondueligans' French-Irish wonderland to the Middle East.

"You fell asleep in the car," Glenn said. "I had to carry you in."

"I hope you didn't hurt your back."

"Don't be silly." He'd put his hair into a man bun that exposed streaks of grey and his model-esque cheek bones. He had sharp, beguiling edges that I hadn't previously noticed.

"What's this music?" I said. My head had cleared a bit. The caffeine was making my heart stutter. My armpits were wet.

"Amal Maher. Top of the charts in Egypt," Glenn said. "I have a particular love for the Middle East."

"Why's that?"

"We lived in Jordan for a few years when I was a child. My dad was in the oil business. But I consider myself a world citizen."

"World citizen? Do explain."

"You told me *you* were a world citizen, well, not in those words. You chanted a Buddhist prayer, spoke a few words in Icelandic, and said you practiced yoga."

"I did?"

"Yes, in the car."

Glenn hopped up, sat next to me, then inched closer. I recognized a new scent: patchouli.

"How do you like the coffee?" he said with a slurp.

"It's good, but my tongue is still a little sore."

I peered into his eyes: he was wearing eyeliner. I had not seen that at Fondueligans. Had he just applied it along with the patchouli? I was starting to feel like myself again, but the uneasiness jumping around in my stomach about his make-up was running interference with my returning equilibrium.

"What kind of candles are these? They smell delicious."

Glenn affected a yawn, then put his arm around me.

"Fig and bergamot," he said. "I use them when I do yoga. Bikram." His voice softened. I could see the outline of his biceps a bit under the shoulders of the scrubs. He seemed fit.

"Want to try something? I've got an aperitif that's killer." I'd had enough to drink, but I couldn't say no to his eyes. Even with the eyeliner, there was something hypnotic, something eerily intoxicating that kept me in his grip.

Glenn clanged around in the kitchen, then returned with two shots of white liquid on a silver tray.

"Cheers." We clinked our tiny glasses.

"Arak," he continued, "is made of anise." He threw his head back and gulped, his Adam's apple protruding through his stubble. I flung my head into my neck and swallowed. The blast of liquorice lit a blue flame of euphoria that raced down my spine and blossomed in my chest.

I held out my glass. "More." Glenn filled me up.

"What kind of crystals are those?" I pointed to a display on his bookcase.

"Well, they're a variety, but mostly ammonite. They exude vitality, life force...confidence. They penetrate your third eye." The liqueur was kicking in and the room began to wobble. I thought I could see his third eye. It winked at me. I jumped.

"What's wrong? You're a nervous, slippery Pisces!"

When did I tell him that?

"But I don't rely on the traditional zodiac. I'm more into Chinese astrology. I'm a rooster. And you, my dear, are a rat."

"That's interesting." My voice cracked, hiding inside my throat.

"Jan, I like you. And I meet lots of women in the classes I teach."

"I thought you were a designer."

"Well," he paused. "I am. I'm a relationship designer.

"What?"

"I teach relationship seminars."

"Really? You're a reNAIssance man," I said. "I like to say it that way because that's the way the Brits do it."

"What?" Glenn's face was as blank as a turnip. He shifted his body to face me. "I teach a continuing education class at Phoenix University, which is an online outfit, but I'm at the brick and mortar down the street. I just finished up a class."

"Huh," I said. "What's the secret to relationships?"

"I follow Adrian Zarov's philosophy," he said. "Compassionate intentionality is the illumination of the cosmic spirit. The transfiguration of cosmic transcendence is the ethereal channel to astral unity. Harmonic convergence is the quantum energy of biofeedback singularity. Universal vibrations connect us all."

"Deep. I think my head just detached from my body." I re-adjusted myself on the couch, uncrossed my legs, which felt very heavy and as I did, my heel came crashing down on his big toe.

"Ouch!"

"I'm sorry."

"I have flat feet and fallen arches." He then took off his sock and began massaging his instep.

"Let me." I caressed his foot, which was surprisingly hairless and smooth.

"That feels amazing." His haunting eyes flashed and the childlike roundness of them started to ignite a feeling in my loins. As I moved closer to him, hoping for a kiss, I burped. A nasty cheesy burp.

"Excuse me! Can I get a soda?"

"Of course."

Glenn sprung into the kitchen. His small, taut buttocks wafted from side to side under his britches like he was smuggling coconuts. While he fetched my beverage, I examined the bric-a-brac on his bookcase.

"Are these fezzes? Is that right? Is that the plural?"

"A fez is a fez is a fez," Glenn yelled from the kitchen. *Was that supposed to be a riddle?*

Glenn handed me a Sprite, changed the music, and went into his room.

"What are you doing?"

"Don't come in!"

The song was livelier, brimming with tambourines and bongos.

Glenn entered the room like a slinky fox, one leg at a time. He was wearing shiny blue, baggy pants that gathered at the ankles. At his waist was a belt of shimmering gold coins. He was shirtless, except for a short, sparkly matching vest that was too small for him: it hit him about mid-chest, only slightly covering his ripe, tawny pecs. On his head was a skull cap with what looked like a dish rag hanging from the back. On his toes, a few rings. In his hands, finger cymbals. As he danced and pranced and spun, his hips moved the opposite direction from his chest, and his stomach contracted and expanded like a toothless mouth. Sequins glittered along the edges of his costume. I tipped back the bottle of Arak, and pounded the rest of it.

He then started doing pelvic thrusts a bit too near to my face.

Darkness.

8 a.m. Panic. I was naked and covered in a scratchy, wool blanket on Glenn's couch. He was in a sleeping bag next to me. My clothes were draped over a chair. *Oh God, we must've had sex.* He had seen my body, my hideous pear-ness. The number of men I'd had sex with appeared like a rolling clock, then ticked over to the next shameful digit. I tiptoed around and got dressed. I could smell the spices from the Arak, along with the meat and cheese from the fondue on my skin; my body heat had cooked them into a horrible perfume.

"Where are you going?" Glenn said, as he rooted around under his covers.

"My meeting is going on *now*. I can't believe this. I need to take you back to your car."

It started to rain and my nausea was acute. The patter of the raindrops and the unforgiving sound of the windshield wipers filled the gap between me and Glenn. I'd grown accustomed to the aching strangeness, the emptiness of the morning after.

Glenn turned on the radio to a jazz station. It was an unstructured number peppered with saxophones that sounded like someone was throwing pots and pans down a stairwell.

"Just can't." I snapped off the radio.

My phone rang. I clicked Accept, then Speaker, but remained silent.

"Jan? Where are you? It's 8:00. I knew you'd pull something like this." It was Sal.

"Sir, I think you have the wrong number," Glenn said in a professorial voice. "But you do sound stressed. Take a deep breath, exhale your negativity, and reach for the cosmic spirit of happiness that connects us all."

"Wha—? Screw you, weirdo."

I hit End on my phone.

"Thanks. I needed that."

"I know," he said. "I know you."

Despite his provocative eyeliner, esoteric philosophies, and spontaneous jig, I was strangely comforted. I could like this man.

"Count Your Blessings"

Mamaw was tired of waiting. Dan, her son, had left her alone again for hours. When he got back, she wanted to tell him to "go lay on the piano," which was what her late husband, Charlie, used to say when he really wanted to say, "go to hell." But she was a good Methodist, and, anyway, they had sold the piano last year to pay long-overdue bills after Dan lost his job at the Boy Scouts.

A painting hung over their couch: a 5 x 5 oil portrait of Dan in a white suit holding a white Bible against a fake backdrop of a bookshelf. He had given it to himself as a present after finishing his online seminary degree and becoming "The Reverend Doctor Dan Nelson." When Dan was five, he had told Mamaw he had been tapped on the shoulder by an angel and been given a special mission by God. He was to be a preacher. Over the years he'd become a member of nearly every church in town. He attended two, sometimes three services on Sunday and a few Bible studies during the week. In the spring, he made it to as many revivals as possible.

Mamaw was hungry and wanted to get out of her threadbare La-Z-Boy, the chair Charlie had died in, and look in the refrigerator, but she'd had hip surgery six weeks ago and couldn't walk. She used to get a shampoo and set at Curly's salon every week, but she was out of money and now her hair hung like strings on her shoulders and her scalp was exposed. And she needed a manicure; her nails were torn and full of hangnails. Her hands moved down her breasts and thighs as she smoothed her purple, tie-dyed caftan, a gift from her hippie granddaughter. She traced her thigh bones with her hands, remembering the fleshy, curvy figure she'd had for decades. At least she had some meat on her fat arms. Still, she'd put on her silver rose lapel pin with sparkling fake diamonds.

She pushed away the TV tray that Dan had set up for her so she could get settled into the chair and start eating the lunch he had laid out: Ensure and weenies. It wasn't really such a bad meal, especially when she poured the Ensure into her coffee cup and dipped the weenies into it. She wished she could have had a nip to go along with her dip. But Dan would go ballistic. How had he gotten to be so *Baptist?*

She grabbed the TV remote, pressed "Power" with her jagged nail, and the sounds of applause from *Wheel of Fortune* filled the room. She was no good at guessing the letters, but it was still exciting to watch people win cash money. And Pat Sajak was nice-looking, though Mamaw wasn't sure he'd ever grown up to be a full-sized man. And he was all one color; his hair matched his skin.

Vanna looked good. Big jugs worked on her. And the revealing evening gown she was wearing made Mamaw think of her own long cocktail dress, the one she'd worn when Dan threw a party for Jane Powell, the big movie star. Dan and Jane had met during one of her Broadway show tours and started to correspond. Mamaw and Charlie were sure they would marry. They had given him thousands of dollars of their hard-earned money for the party and what did they have to show for it?

"Hello, Mama!" Dan called. Mamaw was sure he yelled so loud to see if she was still alive.

"Oh dear! Don't you snick up on me like that! Whew, heart's racing!"

Dan's blue-checked shirt was so wrinkled it looked like he'd slept in it. His Hush Puppies were dirty, and one of them was untied. He had dark circles around his eyes, as if someone had punched him. But what could she expect? Dan was 64 and all his dreams were shattered.

"They wouldn't take these." He dropped a big stack of magazines on the floor—*The Pentecostal Evangel*, *The Texas Trumpet*, and *Cathedral of Light Miracles*.

"The regular guy who buys my magazines wasn't at the bookstore, and the new guy wouldn't take them."

"So I guess this means we don't have any money for food?"

"You SURE there's no weenies left? I thought I saw some in there."

"I ate the last ones for lunch and I'm sick of the Ensure. That's what old people eat. And pull your pants up!"

Dan adjusted his britches, walked into the kitchen and slammed drawers around. Mamaw couldn't hear a word Pat Sajak was saying, but still, the pictures of the cars and Hawaiian vacations were nice to look at. She'd been to every state in the union except Hawaii.

"Well, Mama, you're right," Dan called.

"I'm always right," Mamaw said. "Is Furr's Cafeteria still open? My mouth has been set for their chicken fried steak and cream gravy all day."

"We can't afford that."

"What did you do with the money I gave you the other day?"

"I had to run some errands, put gas in my car," Dan said. "Besides, I don't know if they're still open."

"Can't you call them?"

"Mama, the phone's been cut off."

"Oh, Dan." Mamaw buried her face in her hands. Her fingers clung to her face like claws, then fell to her lap as she looked up. "Well, let's not get all worried now. Count your blessings, not your troubles. That's my motto."

"Maybe they're still open," Dan said. "I'll get your coat."

Dan was going to have to move her from her chair to her wheelchair. And she was afraid he'd drop her. Though he was a big man, he wasn't strong.

"Okay, you ready?" Dan reached under her armpits and raised her up, but she winced, wriggled away from him, and plopped back down.

"Your fingers are hurting me! Use your whole hand."

"On the count of three," Dan said.

Mamaw looked up at Dan and examined his odd-shaped head. "One of your ears lobes is longer than the other."

"Mama, I'm well aware of that," Dan said. "Okay: one, two, three." He lifted her up and into the wheelchair.

"You forgot the brake!" Mamaw cried.

Dan clicked the brake into place and stepped back. "There. I'll be right back."

Dan walked into his room and shut the door. Mamaw adjusted her bottom in the seat of the wheelchair and stuffed Dan's jacket around her like a blanket. Then she heard Dan praying. It sounded like he was channeling a goat. He had told Mamaw that a man at his healing church had his stump restored to a full arm, and a woman had her nub turned into a full finger. Every time he told her these stories, he smiled wide. His toothless gums were wet, pink, and gleaming. Mamaw had no teeth, either. She'd had dentures until Dan dropped them on the floor and the two front teeth fell out.

When Dan walked back into the living room, he was sweating and his eyes were wild. "Let's go," he said. He clasped his hands, stretched them out in front of him and cracked his knuckles.

"I've told you that's annoying," Mamaw said.

"Nobody's perfect."

Dan pushed her out to their old Dodge Dart—he called it *his* car, but she'd bought it years ago; she didn't have the heart to correct him. Dan had suffered mightily. He hadn't held a steady job since he had lived in D.C. and got fired after he told his boss to stop cussing. When he came back home to Dallas, he said he'd been blackballed from every job in America. He then plunged himself into genealogy and corresponded with long-lost third and fourth cousins. He told Mamaw they were related to George Washington, Thomas Jefferson, and Jesus Christ. Mamaw and Charlie got a good laugh out of that.

"Okay," Dan said. "Hold on to my neck. I need to scoot you over into the seat. Just let your legs go limp."

Mamaw was holding on tight to his neck, but it was slippery with sweat.

"Did you put on any Old Spice?" she said. "You smell a bit ripe."

"Just hang on, will you?"

She prayed to Jesus that she'd make it into the car. After a quick heave-ho, she was in and they were off.

Dan narrated as he drove along the interstate. "Kurt's Automotive. *He's good people.* Cluckin' Chicken. *Love their spicy nuggets.*"

Bendy's Salt Water Taffy came into view. "Wonder how those folks are since you left that job," Mamaw said. In high school, Dan had been fired from Bendy's for throwing a pan at the manager. Dan turned on the radio to a Christian station. Some man was singing "How Great Thou Art," as if his throat was clogged with socks.

"Turn that off," Mamaw said. "That song makes my gums hurt."

Dan snapped the radio off.

"I sure do like Furr's chocolate icebox pie," Mamaw said. "I hope they have a slice left."

When they pulled up to Furr's, the lights were still on and Mamaw could see a few figures walking around inside. Dan got out and walked up to the door, but it wouldn't open. He shook his head, then with his pointer finger drew an "X" on the CLOSED sign—he'd put a hex on it. Mamaw had gotten used to Dan's hexing things he didn't approve of. When he watched the Dallas Cowboys play and they were losing, he put a hex on the head of the opposing team's coach. Walked right up to the screen and hexed him good.

"They closed at 7," Dan said, as he shut the car door.

"What'll we do?" Mamaw said. "I've run out of food stamps. Are we going to the soup kitchen?"

"Mama, I'm going to take care of you. I always do," Dan said. "I've got a surprise."

Dan tore out of the parking lot and Mamaw looked at the speedometer. He was definitely driving over the limit. She started to say something, but didn't. When they reached the Linwood Mall, he turned into a parking lot full of expensive cars. Dan squeezed their Dart next to a navy-blue Jaguar and she saw the sign: Temple Shalom. "What in the world are we doing here?"

"Tonight's a Bat Mitzvah," Dan said. "I heard some people talking about it last Friday night at Shabbat services and there's probably a big buffet."

"I'm not going in there. We could have at least gone to the other places you go to: Second Methodist Church. The Christian Science Reading Room, one of those other places on your religious Lazy Susan."

"That was ugly, Mama."

"I'm sorry." There was a large, heavy pain inside Mamaw that was too big for her spirit. She tried to push it away, store it underneath her grief for Charlie. She tried to visualize putting it inside her jewelry box, or between the pages of her Bible, but it kept insisting to be seen and heard. She folded her hands and said a quick prayer, "Lord, help us."

Dan grabbed the rear-view mirror and smoothed his hair, then pointed to her feet. "House shoes?"

"You didn't say we were going to the prom!" Mamaw's feet were comfy in her slippers. There was a hole that exposed her big toe. She gave it a wiggle.

"Can you at least put on some lipstick?"

She pulled down the visor and realized he was right. Her lips looked white and cracked and old—she was old!—and needed a spot of color. As she was putting on her favorite shade, Love That Red by Mary Kay, she felt Dan's fingers on her shoulder fiddling with her shimmering pin. He was always trying to fix her clothes or fluff her hair. She wanted to turn him over her knee like she should have done when he was a little boy. He might have amounted to something by now. But Charlie always said to leave him be.

"This whole thing would make your daddy cry," she said. She held on to Dan's neck as he got her into her wheelchair.

The lights were bright in the ballroom and a big disco ball was hanging from the ceiling casting sparkly lights all around. Mamaw heard the clinking and clattering of silverware, along with the voices and music. The room smelled like rich people, perfumed and clean, and the rich people were staring at them. She wished Dan had magic powers to teleport them out of the room and move them through the door, like Jesus did the morning of the third day.

Young folks were standing in circles visiting, as they did at the Methodist church. Lots of people were hugging. Everyone was attractive— dark-headed and dark-eyed. Everyone knew everyone.

"The Jews are a beautiful people," Mamaw said. "I'm Black Irish and could have passed for a Jew years ago."

"Sssshhh!" Dan pushed her over to one of the tables that lined the dance floor. It all smelled delicious; she felt a little less hungry just inhaling. There was a big slab of roast beef under a hot light and silver dishes with lids. She wondered what was inside. Then she felt a stabbing pain in her stomach like the way she did after she ate tomatoes.

"I need some water," she said. Dan ran off into the crowd. Mamaw's hips were vibrating because the music was so loud. She had a flash, a memory, of dancing with Charlie at Dan's big party. She moved her stick ankles gently, as if she were trying to do the box step, then stopped when it got too painful. To avoid any eye contact she started to examine her fingernails.

"It's time to celebrate Jenny!" a man called into a microphone. He was wearing a Cat in the Hat hat. A pretty young girl in a light blue dress appeared and then a bunch of men picked her up on a chair and paraded her around the room. The girl didn't look a bit pleased. The chair was tilted. Mamaw couldn't look because she thought the girl was going to fall. *Where in the hell was Dan?*

Now everyone was holding hands and dancing in a circle. The song that played was in a minor key and sad. Mamaw saw a group of girls whispering and looking at her. Maybe she hadn't put on her lipstick correctly. Maybe it was her tie-dyed caftan. She put her hands on the wheels of her chair and tried to roll herself over to the roast beef, but her arms just didn't work like they used to.

A man in a little round hat came up behind Mamaw and pushed her out to the dance floor and started spinning her in a circle. He was drunk. He bent down and gave her a wink. *Did he think she was pretty?* He must not be able to see very well—his glasses were awful thick. Now more men were dancing around her clapping and smiling. She felt someone kick her wheelchair and she thought she was going to fall out. Someone spilled champagne on her head.

"STOP! STOP!" she shouted, but they kept kicking up their legs and twisting their hips.

Finally Mamaw saw Dan—*Thank you Lord!*—and he wheeled her back out of the crowd. She could have grabbed one of the steak knives on the table and given him a poke.

"WHY DID YOU LEAVE ME?" She was hoarse from yelling at the men.

Dan shoved the wheelchair towards the roast beef and cut in line.

He put a plate in her lap and helped her fill it with mashed potatoes and some mushy green vegetable. By the time they reached the meat man, Mamaw was so hungry she could have eaten his big fat hand that was carving the bloody block of animal.

As Dan pushed her toward an empty table, she stabbed her fork into the red, juicy slab and took a bite. Sometimes it was good to wait to eat for a long time because things tasted extra delicious in her mouth.

There were a few purses, half-filled glasses and plates on the white tablecloth; the people must have been dancing. Oh my, did those mashed potatoes taste divine! She spotted a bar across the room and craved a glass of wine; however, that wasn't going to happen. Dan asked that they pray over the food; but Mamaw pretended she didn't hear him.

"Hello there! I'm Judy Kimmel, Jenny's aunt. I'm sorry, remind me of how you know Jenny?" Judy was a slim, athletic, middle-aged woman in a shiny green dress, with short dark hair and a string of pearls around her neck. She looked very educated.

"I was at Shabbat services Friday night," Dan said. "They told me there was a party, and that everyone was invited." His eyes were cloudy, confused— panicked. Mamaw had seen that look when he was five years old when she was teaching him to tie his shoe.

"Well," Judy said. "That's not exactly right. But please, make yourselves at home."

Dan sat up straight and wiped the corners of his mouth. "Thank you kindly, I'm Dan. And this is my mother, Linda. Are you with Mixed Nuts? The singles' group? I've been to some of the events."

"No, I'm not."

"I see you're not wearing a ring. You married?"

"I'm a widow."

Judy leaned down to Mamaw and perfume crept into her nose: Chanel No. 5. It was a scent she had worn as a young woman. "I like your jazzy outfit." She patted Mamaw on the shoulder. Her hand was heavy. It lingered on her back, then slipped away.

"JESUS CHRIST, DAN," Mamaw said. "I've had enough."

"Thou shalt not take the Lord's name in vain," Dan said. Mamaw put her fork down on her plate and sat back in her chair. The noise of the crowd faded away.

"Honor Thy Mother and Thy Father. And stop sucking on scripture like a titty! I want a glass of wine."

Dan stared into Mamaw's face as if he didn't know her, then hurried away, and pushed in front of people at the bar. He walked back fast, his ham-sized thighs pressed together, as if he had to go to the bathroom.

"Here's your wine," he said, thrusting a glass of red wine into her face.

Dan sat down and stared into the carpet. Mamaw swirled her wine around on her tongue. She licked her lips and took another sip. The sharp, warm goodness reminded her of the days when Charlie was alive, before Dan was born, when they had joy in their lives.

"Thank you," Mamaw said. "Now we can go."

Dan dropped two crescent rolls in Mamaw's purse, snapped it shut and pushed her out into the cool night air.

"Summer, 1979"

Baby oil is slathered all over my white, starchy skin. A prism of ooze on my arms is washed with sweat. My legs are outstretched on a beach towel. They go on for centuries. I'm still, a statue worshipping the sun in the backyard. I've never felt more alive.

Ruddy snuck into my room last night. He shimmied up the trellis, then slipped in through my window. We got into my bed and it hurt. I didn't think it would, but it did. I'd heard it might be tight and it was, but I could stand the pain. My skin prickles and my stomach feels weird, probably just hunger.

Dishes clang, the TV is on, and we dig in. Utensils chime in the stunning silence.

You seem sleepy, Mom says.

I'm not.

I heard you get up last night. I heard footsteps.

I was just going to the bathroom. More beans, please.

Are you sure?

Of course!

You woke me up. Don't chew with your mouth open.

I need some of that aloe. Can you give me some after I shower?

Tomorrow we need to go to the DMV to get your learner's permit. I can't keep driving you to school.

Mom passes me watermelon, her summer standard. It's gash red. I try to avoid the seeds, but I chomp down anyway and the sweetness bathes my tongue, exploding, juice waterfalling down my chin. I eat with abandon and I can't stop. *More, more, more.*

My hair is getting longer and I wash it. I let it drip dry and slip into my shorts.

Mom, I'm ready.

She joins me on the couch and I push my strap down. The small aloe leaf is gooey and cool and her hands feel like love.

You've got to wear sunscreen.

No I don't. I like to get tanned.

The screen door slams behind me and the yard is lousy with fireflies. They dance, just beyond my grasp. They're so free and magical. I am one of them. I close my eyes and move with abandon, jettisoning into the unknown, sailing away, eating air, devouring the nebulas.

The night is quiet. A few cars pass by. The cicadas are blasting away, a welcome chorus for June. Cool grass massages my feet, a velvet carpet for living. In the corner under an ancient oak, I light up a Marlboro Red I have tucked into my bra. The nicotine razors my throat. I exhale my truth. *I have big dreams.* Beyond the branches, there's a half-moon, a slice of apple, marbleized white. Two stars above it make a face, but there's no nose.

It's time to burn myself again. Not gonna break my pact with Sandra. I hide the scars in my armpit. I've made a cross and need just one more to complete it. The butt glows like the red planet, it hovers over my flesh, then a sharp sting. *I am dangerous.*

#

The low part of my tummy just above my privates is all puffy and hurty. I probably ate too many Jolly Ranchers. I stole a ton from Sandra during gym. I broke into her locker. I crave them. My period is supposed to come; I hate the way I feel before, all bloated and cranky and headachy.

#

Dear God or Jesus or Whoever's in charge, I'll never have sex again. I'm scared to the pi power. I push my boobs together with my wrists and yep, they're sore, ready to nurse, but then again, I'll just wait it out. Periods and being pregnant, I've read, feel the same. Aunt Flo will visit, Mom always says. *So stupid.*

#

The line is pink.

#

We used a rubber, Ruddy says. Oh God, this can't be, this can't be happening.
  It might have busted, I say.
  I'll go with you to the doctor, the clinic. I love you.
  I love you, too, but I gotta go. Mom's gotta use the phone.

#

High school drop out? Wear the scarlet letter? Work at Church's Fried Chicken? I can't even make change. I suck at math. I need this alien to go away, this baby, this thing, this membrane. It's part of me, and then it's not. I read in a women's history book that there are ways to do this.

I want to move away or burrow into the ground and pop up in China. My teeth are chattering. I've been in my room all day, door shut, Dan Fogelberg album playing over and over, and I've been painting my toenails. *This can't be.* My voice wallpapers my brain and the sound becomes a whisper.

#

My bag is packed. Cigarettes, check. Heaven Sent, Mom's perfume, check. More Jolly Ranchers, check. Sandra would never know it was me. Mom's passed out on the couch drinking Chablis and watching TV and last I looked, her cookbook was open on her lap.

I'm leaving now, I say. You'll see me flash my lights at the corner.

I'm not coming, Ruddy says.

You said you would.

I lied.

The bottom of the stairs is a galaxy away. I'm not sure I can do it. Just do a somersault. Pretend to faint. Fake a seizure.

I fling myself down, sharp edges knife my head, my ribs, my legs. Pain shotguns through every cell, *come on blood, come on blood.* Hope blossoms amidst the disaster of mom's approaching footsteps.

###

"The Light of Day"

George returned from his morning walk and heard a shrill sound from the upstairs condo.

"Idiots!" he muttered. He would have to complain again.

A bachelor, George liked peace and quiet. He noticed a sliver of light peeking around the blackout shade. He smoothed it into place and made his way upstairs. His back ached, his knees creaked, and his body formed a question mark. He adjusted his sunglasses and patted his toupee, something he thought of as dentures for the head.

On the way out, he straightened a photograph taken at the Olan Mills Portrait Studio. A woman with blue-gray hair in a jacket and white blouse sat ramrod straight. A tall man in a suit and tie stood behind, a hand on her shoulder. The pose was stiff, but a good likeness of George and his mother.

"The bright flash hurts my eyes," she said. She disliked having her picture taken. She allowed George to drive her to the mall, but the wily photographer could not make her smile.

Thirty years ago when the condo complex was new, George and his widowed mother were some of the first residents to move in. It was a "mature singles" place, located in a prime spot in Dallas. Everyone had to be over 50, and children were not allowed. The management made an exception for George, who was 29 at the time. He claimed to be his mother's caretaker.

"She's forgetful," he'd said. "She often leaves the house with the stove on." They'd gotten by on her Social Security, a nest egg from the departed, and his job at Klovis Elevators.

A repair technician, he endured abuse from impatient office workers and apartment dwellers.

"What goes up must come down," he often said. George wanted to scream at them, or slap the worst offenders. His mother said, "You just need to toughen up."

Shortly after she died, George retired. Without meaning to, he slid into mourning. He believed he was hypersensitive to sound and light.

He banged on the upstairs neighbor's door.

"Hi, George." Eleanor inched the door open. She was an apple-shaped older woman of mysterious sorrows. She wore a robe and padded slippers. Beyond sat a barefoot woman, perhaps in her 20s, cradling a sleek electric guitar.

"The noise is making my teeth hurt!" George's voice shot into a higher register.

"I'm so sorry." Eleanor was ruffled. "I thought getting these thick rugs would help. I take my shoes off every time I get home."

"That's fine, but it isn't working. The noise has been going on for over a year, and now this!" He cut his eyes towards the woman.

"Vicky is getting ready for her gig this evening," Eleanor said. "She plays guitar at a coffee house."

George was suspicious. Musicians couldn't be trusted.

"Vicky," Eleanor said, "this is George."

"Sorry if my tuning was too loud." Vicky nodded, not looking in any particular direction. Her fingers crabbed toward the volume dial on her amplifier, and she turned it down. "There."

Eleanor inched close to George. "She's my new roommate. I'm trying to save money."

"That's fine," George said, and stepped back. She always spoke too close. "Nice to see you," he said to Vicky.

"Wish I could say the same." Vicky giggled, exposing her moist gums. Her eyes rolled back in her head when she talked. She was blind.

George was struck by how small Vicky was, diminutive. She resembled a little boy. Her short hair cupped her face, and her eyelashes fluttered when she spoke. Despite his irritation with her playing, he wanted to fold her up and put her in a pocket. But he pushed those feelings away.

The last time he felt something like this was in high school. He'd asked a girl for a date, and she laughed in his face. Then, when he was in the shower after basketball practice, he became attracted to a fellow player and felt guilty. The feelings didn't go away. In an attempt to thwart his obsession, he wore a thick rubber band around his left wrist. Every time the basketball boy entered his mind, he snapped it.

"I respect your talent," George said to Vicky. "But if you could play more quietly, I'd appreciate it."

"If I don't practice, I won't be any good. I won't keep my gig, and I need money for rent, so I must practice. Have you tried ear plugs?"

"I can't tolerate anything in my ears," George said.

"How about your fingers?" Eleanor said. She jammed her forefingers in each of her ears.

"We've talked about this," George said. "And I've talked to Frank."

Frank, Eleanor's landlord, was a forty-something man on his fourth marriage. He had a bad complexion, and he smelled like an ashtray with a top note of Pine Sol. When George complained to him, he replied, "Suck it up, old man."

"I'll find a practice space," Vicky said. "I want to be a good neighbor."

George was ashamed. Prickly discomfort sluiced through his veins. When people did nice things for him, there was always a catch.

"My car's not working," Eleanor said, "so I need to split. Gotta help

Vicky navigate the bus tonight."

"I can drive her," George said, surprised at his own response. An awkward, cozy sensation of kindness settled around his shoulders, like one of his mother's knitted shawls.

#

Vicky would be ready to leave in an hour. George went downstairs and disrobed for a sponge bath. He didn't like being totally naked when he bathed. When George showered, he wore his underwear. The force of the water hurt.

He applied deodorant, squirted drops in his eyes, and put on a fresh shirt. He combed his hairpiece. He slipped into his walking shoes, inside of which were orthotics for his plantar fasciitis. He put on his dark glasses.

When George opened his door, Vicky was already there. She wore a purple dress and a scarf. Her guitar case in the crook of an elbow, an amplifier like a suitcase on wheels. With the other hand, she held her cane, her fingers laced through the plastic loop.

"Oh! You gave me a start!" George said.

Vicky laughed, her pink lips gleamed. "I like to surprise people."

As they baby-stepped down the irregular pavement of the driveway to the car, George carried her guitar case and warned her of uneven spots. Vicky swung her cane from side to side and swatted him across the shins.

"You get around well for a blind person," George said.

"Thanks, you get around well for a fake blind person."

"What?"

"Eleanor told me you wear sunglasses so people will think you can't see."

"I have tender retinas," George said. "And sensitive ears and skin."

"I'm just blind. Thanks for being a pal." She reached over and patted his shoulder. She squeezed his hand. He pulled his shirt sleeve down to hide the rubber band.

George flung open the door to his SUV, but Vicky couldn't navigate the elevated step. He placed his hands on her hips and lifted her inside. He thought he could feel her skin through her thin blouse, and he shivered.

It had been a long time since he'd touched someone's flesh. He once dated a radiation technician, Dennis, for a year. But Dennis had cheated on him with Sally, the office manager. He wondered what a relationship with a woman might be like. Rowdy thoughts invaded George's head. His neck beaded with sweat.

As they drove, he narrated to take his mind off the discomfort that pressed in.

"Right now, we've just passed Like New Dry Cleaners, Lug Nuts Auto, and Chubby's Restaurant. Now I'm going to accelerate onto the interstate."

George squeezed the steering wheel and drove under the speed limit. An angry driver blew past them and laid on the horn.

#

When they arrived in Garland, George announced the name of the coffee house.

"Lots of Perks. That's a joke," he said, but Vicky didn't seem to hear him.

As they walked in, George guided Vicky by the arm.

"Excuse us," he said, as customers stared and backed up to let them pass. George relished the extra attention and intentionally bumped into chairs. One fell over with a bang. Heads turned, and more people got out of their way. After he righted the chair with apologies to the crowd, they made their way to a table up front, not far from the stage.

"Here you go," George said. He helped Vicky get seated and opened her guitar case.

"Don't forget the amp," Vicky said.

"Let's get you hooked up." George removed the speaker from Vicky's rolling cart, hoisted it up on stage, and moved her chair into position.

Customers trickled in. A carrot-haired man with a curly-cue moustache and his handsome wife in a pantsuit. A middle-aged woman with a short gray haircut and baggy Walmart jeans. A healthy-looking couple in their twenties who looked like they always took their vitamins and never passed gas.

"What'll it be?" a waiter said, his pen poised above his small pad.

"Hi, Bubba," Vicky said. "Coffee, please, black with honey."

George raised his chin and tipped his head back to shore up his disabled façade. "Vicky told me the cappuccino was good. I'll have that."

"Okay," Bubba said, his brows furrowed, suspect of George's affliction.

George helped Vicky get situated onstage. As he bent down, his glasses fell off, skittered across the floor, and stopped short at the waiter's feet.

"Here you go," Bubba said. He set down the drinks and picked up George's glasses. He held them between his thumb and forefinger, as if they smelled bad.

The waiter had a high-pitched voice and a swishy manner. The gesture of disdain irritated George. Something like fury boiled in his stomach and ricocheted up his esophagus. Bubba reminded him of his mother.

George rolled his eyes back and extended his palm to receive the glasses. He muttered a terse thank-you. He grumbled as he put them back on, then crossed his arms over his chest.

As Vicky tuned her guitar, she closed her eyes in ecstasy. Her long eyelashes ticked and jiggled, as she explored her instrument. George watched and winced. But as Vicky continued, the sharp sounds became pleasing. Then, with one glorious strum, the music started.

Vicky bent close to her guitar, her body leaning forward then back, expanding and contracting like a lung. George swayed in harmony and hummed along. His fingers found his rubber band, and he massaged his wrist. The more Vicky played, the more her face glistened. Her skin was porcelain. The minor chords of the bluesy ballad unearthed a faraway longing inside George. The soft luminescence of the chandelier was magical. George thought for a moment that Vicky was translucent.

On the way home, George turned off the radio. "I have a present for you."

"I love presents."

"It's not much, but here you go."

He pulled over on a side street. He removed his sunglasses and blinked in the twilight. Carefully, he placed the sunglasses on Vicky's face.

"My shades look better on you than on me."

"You're funny. I don't need these. People already know that I'm blind." She removed the sunglasses and dropped them in her lap.

George's chest fell, as if he'd given her a flower that suddenly wilted.

"Those were a special pair my mother gave me the Christmas before she passed. They were expensive."

"Do you really need them?" Vicky caressed the lenses.

"The ultraviolet rays are killing my eyes. I have an eroded cornea over my pupil, and the sclera is thin, the white of the eye."

"Are you sure?"

"Yes, I'm sure! I've been to many doctors. Several said they couldn't find anything wrong. Finally, one doctor ran a series of tests. He explained to me about the retina, the cornea, and the sclera."

"You're stronger than you think you are, George."

"Do you think so?"

"Yes. You are." She reached for George, missed, then found his shoulder and gave it a pat. "You just can't see it."

#

After the performance at the coffee house, George's distress about the racket upstairs was replaced with anticipation. Every footstep he heard overhead was Vicky's, he imagined. He tried to squelch his desire with the rubber band.

George became Vicky's driver. They began to enjoy regular outings: trips to the park, concerts, even church. George still went to the Presbyterian church his family joined many years ago. Wherever they went, they hooked arms, so Vicky wouldn't run into things. Once George grabbed Vicky's hand to keep her from taking a fatal step into oncoming traffic. Her hand was soft as a baby's, yet her fingertips were rough. He wanted to stroke them, but restrained himself. The texture of her calluses haunted him. It reminded him of the surface of a basketball.

#

One evening, George and Vicky entered the condo complex and were met with a veil of smoke. It was Frank, with a cigarillo. Vicky bent forward and coughed.

"Hey, can you put that out?" George said. He coughed, too.

"I'm okay," Vicky said. She rubbed her nose.

"Free country, George," Frank said.

"But being a jerk will cost you," George said.

"Is that a threat?" Frank said.

"Are you here to work on my sink, Frank?" Vicky interrupted.

"Excuse us," George guided Vicky upstairs to her front door, where she fiddled with her keys.

"Kitchen sink's all fixed," Frank shouted from below.

"Go away," George said. Vicky let herself in. George turned on his heel, his eyes cast downward, and stomped down the stairs.

#

A week later, after they'd finished a buffet at a neighborhood cafeteria, George and Vicky arrived home. He parked in the fire lane next to the common grassy area, so they'd be closer to their building.

"Hey, you can't park in the fire lane. I've asked you not to do this before," a voice said. It was Frank.

"Excuse me?" George said.

"I didn't know you favored the ladies," Frank muttered behind his back.

"Say that to my face!" George clenched his fists.

Frank's eyes bulged, his nostrils flared like a prize bull, and he marched towards George.

"Relax, George!" Vicky yelled. She extended her cane in front of her, gesticulated, as if it were a long finger cutting the air.

"Aahh!" Frank cried, as he tripped over the stick.

Vicky tumbled down. Her cane clattered on the pavement. She rolled from side to side, mumble-moaned, and hugged her chest.

Frank scrunched his face, palmed his brow as a scarlet stream trickled into his eye.

"You moron!" George said.

He rushed to Vicky. His toupee flapped like a loose shingle, detached, and landed on the grass. He cradled her in his arms and regarded her face. Her cheeks were like pearls. Her eyes were wide, lost and scared. Her hands searched the lawn as if they were hungry.

"Are you hurt? Vicky? Talk to me."

"I'm fine."

George was invigorated. He yanked off his sunglasses and flung them on the pavement. They shattered and split in half.

"You mean man!" George screamed, as he stood over Frank. He clutched Vicky's cane and whipped him. "Say you're sorry!"

"I'm sorry," Frank mumbled.

"Louder!" George jabbed Frank in the stomach.

"I'm sorry!"

Vicky struggled to rise. George swooped in and scooped her up. She was light as a butterfly. Warmed up now, his muscles flexed, he was strong.

"Don't mess with me again!" George yelled.

"Put me down," Vicky said.

George set her on her feet and returned the cane to her hand. He brushed the grass from her clothes, and made sure to remove every blade until she was immaculate.

"George, are you okay?" Vicky said. "George?"

"Let's go," George said firmly, his mouth as straight as a line.

#

That night, the digital display of George's alarm clock lit up his bedroom. The blackout shades caused it to feel like a dungeon. Even though he wore a sleep mask, the blood-red numbers kept him awake. His mind was unruly, obsessed. Shame about the way he harmed Frank ate its way through his brain, gobbling up who he thought he was: a nice, nervous guy who had tried to live a decent life. He felt his mother's presence in the room, but he knew she wasn't there. He covered his face with a pillow and shrieked. The bedding muffled his outburst, and he slept.

At dawn, George awoke. He sprang out of bed. The air in the room was tight. As if possessed, he ripped the heavy fabric from the windows. Warm sunlight flooded the bedroom. He opened his eyes wide and stared at the fiery star on the horizon. From now on, he would live by the light of day.

"Dirty Laundry"

I pour bleach over the mound, purging, once again, the family secret: Daddy's arrest—*indecent exposure*. Socks fall in. Slipped them off right before having sex with my husband, during which I thought of Benjamin, high school lover.

Will Mom die today? Bed sore as big as a baseball. Not eating or drinking. Been seven days. Hampton Gardens is five minutes away, thank Christ. Flannel nightgown, *shove it in*, hope I don't have another nightmare where I'm digging into my giant thigh with a knife, the insides like a Christmas ham.

I told Mom I loved her, that she was the best Mama in the whole world, then I put Chapstick on her faded lips and kissed her papery forehead. New jeans, squeezed my watermelon-ass into them. I'm starving, that Three-Day Cabbage Diet didn't work. *For better, for worse, you said.* T-shirt from Beverly Hills, all the famous people don't smell or fart. Their parents never die.

Daddy, Mama will see you soon. Dishrag smells like ripe lady parts, salmon was a bust, stupid Martha Stewart. *Mama screamed and clawed my wrist, 'please help me, please help me' so I ran and got the nurse who gave her a drop of morphine. Please God, take me instead, I did have that affair.* Next: bath towel, the expensive one from Peacock Alley. *The plush speaks to my skin and says I will go on living.*

Squirt, squirt. Liquid detergent syrups the clothes, in goes the whitening pod that never works, but I'm an optimist, damn it. Phone rings.

Her breathing is ragged, shallow, her heart rate has dropped. Come now.

"The Sister from Nestor"

Last night, I dreamt I was the Sister from Nestor with punk pigs, a homely farm girl who was crazy nuts about piggies. Sister was the nickname a gay friend of mine had. Father gave it to him. Nestor is the last name of an impossibly hot, Viking-ish frat guy in college. Punk because I've been listening to the Ramones, like nonstop. The pigs factor in because I have strict kosher Jewish neighbors.

#

I woke up singing the Sister from Nestor with punk pigs, as if it were a well-known, get-stuck-up-in-your-craw commercial jingle, when I was on a trip with mom in Austin to hear Russell Crowe's band sing, TOFOG. Thirty Odd Foot of Grunts—*hear this in a Kiwi accent.* Grunts, like the film soundtrack term, as opposed to snorts or farts or toots. TOFOG played country songs with furrowed-brow vocals by King Russell and raging, jangly guitars, but not punk.

#

If I did have pigs I would adorn them with '80s Soho London punk snout rings, tattoos of *Babe*, and hurty-to-the eyes hot pink Mohawks. My dad did hair but would never agree to give anyone a Mohawk. He did shampoos and sets and finger pin curls. He wasn't gay but once someone scratched "FAG" on his car door. It killed me. He died in a car wreck, drunk driver, a few months after mom met Russell.

#

I don't have a sister but was in a sorority, so I guess I do have sisters. I'm not married and don't have children. I'm a dead end DNA.

#

Mom is dead now. She met Russell once after a concert. She shook his hand and vowed to never wash it. Her bones dream of him.

#

Lots of girls I knew were sexually assaulted by frat guys. Especially the frat that was known for coke users and that didn't admit blacks or Jews.

#

Mom finally washed her hand after she burned it while frying pork chops she was making for dad. He had a heart attack several days later before he was struck dead by the drunk. Was on his way to CVS to buy his beta blockers. Right before he left, he'd combed mom's mahogany hair and sprayed it until it was hard like a shellacked wedding cake.

#

I was assaulted but not by a frat guy. My perp was a bartender who served me five shots of Jägermeister and shaved me down there and I got stubbles for weeks. Wearing pants was hell. I sued him but lost. *Swine.*

#

Joey Ramone is dead, too. And Jewish. I always wished I was a Member of the Tribe. My kosher neighbors' son said he didn't eat bacon in the house. Only out of the house at Denny's with his Hebrew school friends.

#

Writing just after you wake up is like dumping out a messy kitchen drawer. Nothing matches but somehow it all goes together.

###

"Reunion"

Patrick wanted to melt into the dirty, plaid industrial carpet in the La Quinta ballroom. That, or vomit—the smells were hideous, a combination of overcooked roast beef, body odor, and sulphur. He didn't like the people in high school then, those who were nested around him now, and he wondered why on earth he thought he'd want to see them again, especially Alison, who he'd run into at the pasta bar. It was as if she was following him.

"So catch me up on you," Alison said. A short bespectacled woman with a frizz of red curls, she stared at Patrick with a strange gleam in her eyes and slurped her martini as it waterfalled over the sides of her glass.

Patrick gave her a quick up-and-down glance. *She's really blimped out.* Guilt coursed through his corpus. *Bad Patrick.* A picture formed in his mind of Alison years ago marching along with the flag corps on the AstroTurf with her cohorts in what looked like a policeman's uniform. In the mists of Patrick's memory, she padded along, high-stepping and clad in culottes and knee socks, instead of the usual heavily starched pants the guys donned. His lips tried to conceal a snicker.

"Do you talk to Thom?" she said in a loud, grating voice.

Patrick's stomach tightened and he folded into himself. "Nah."

An ample, brunette woman in a green pantsuit waddled onto a small stage and positioned herself in front of the microphone.

"Really?" Alison said.

"Sssshh," Patrick said.

"Good evening Wolverines!" It was the class president, Nadine, who was now a dentist. In back of her hung a large sign that said, "Welcome Wolverines Class of 1988" trimmed in black and red balloons.

"If you haven't signed in with your phone number and email, please see Donny at the front door. Let's give it up for Donny!" Donny, a slim Jewish guy dressed in overly formal clothing, a tux, jumped up, and flailed his hand and shouted something unintelligible.

"First off, I want to thank everyone who showed up. We weren't sure if all you rock stars would want to come back to our little gathering, but so glad you did!"

Patrick surveyed the expressions of his classmates around him. Most were as blank as paper bags.

"I thought we'd kick off the event by having the cheerleaders come up and lead us in a cheer!"

A flurry of limbs, arms and legs in motion, hands over mouths in mock embarrassment, merged into a string of girls who push-dragged each other up to the stage. Patrick's stomach twisted. He knew those faces, faces who'd mocked him in high school for being Mr. Wolverine, the mascot, and the same faces who spread vicious rumors about him.

Why did I buy into the crap that people at work told me, that the nerds like me were the ones who everyone would be jealous of, that things would be different? I mean, heck, I'm the CEO of Plant Town! I have over 30 direct reports!

The cheerleaders formed a line. They pulled down their too-short sparkly dresses over their enlarged thighs and swung their hands around and clutched their wine glasses like prizes. Patrick was gutted by the way he saw himself in high school: a big, jiggly dork. He was struck with the unassailable truth that he'd made a mistake coming, so while the girls were chittering he skulked away.

"PATRICK GODFREY! COME BACK! WE NEED MR. WOLVERINE!" The voices were shrill and overlapped. Patrick's legs stopped and cemented into the carpet. The lure of their compliments, compliments he wanted to believe, paralyzed him. As if led by Svengali, he wheeled around and trudged toward the stage.

"Yay! Patrick!!! Woot, woot!" A few whistles rippled behind him.

"Okay, okay," Patrick said. He shooed them away, deflecting their adulation.

"Grrrrrr, Grrrr!" Patrick growled, fist-pumped into the air and jogged to the stage, drenched in an intoxicating brew of fear and exhilaration. He stumbled up the main step—his new boots were wooden and hurty. The crowd still roared.

Nadine was bent over a box wrestling with something inside. As she turned, Patrick saw it in her clutches: his Wolverine head.

"Put it on!" Nadine cried.

Patrick's face flamed. Every cell revolted. Senior year, he'd left it in the gym and hoped to never see it again.

"Where did you—?"

"I saved it."

"No, please, no. I can't."

"Oh, come on!"

Patrick heaved a sigh, wriggled his head into the paper mache, furry helmet, zipped it up the back, and there he was: Mr. Wolverine.

Everything from high school came back to him: the unsteady weight of the head and small eyeholes. The air was tight, but by gum, he was going to give it his all.

"Let's go Wolverines, let's go!" Clap, clap. "Let's go Wolverines, let's go!" Patrick shouted. The cheerleaders joined in his revelry and swayed back and forth. One of them who wore conspicuously high heels performed a hurky and landed perfectly. Her blonde, shellacked hair helmet didn't move an inch.

As the stage emptied and the crowd dissolved, Patrick floated off the stage. He started to unzip his Wolverine head, but got distracted. *Looking good, Patrick! You're awesome, man! Rock it, Patrick!* Glimpses of toothy, wide-mouthed smiles and compliments kept coming his way as he made his way out of the ballroom. What once was borderline embarrassing, being the mascot, now seemed to be a status symbol. *Guess my work peeps were right.* All through the night, people seemed to be glad to see him. The head cheerleader even said to him, "You were popular." Popular? He wanted to believe it was true, but in a muscle lodged somewhere near his heart, a belief thrummed: it was all a lie.

In the distance, Patrick spotted Alison elbowing her way through the crowd toward him, so he picked up his pace to escape her, but someone patted him on the back.

"Dude!"

It was Thom.

Thom stepped forward, and extended his hand and they shook. Patrick was surprised to see him clad in khakis, a business shirt, and navy jacket, primed and ready for the top 2%. In high school, he was all Dead Head t-shirts, Birkenstocks, and whiffs of patchouli.

"It's been a while." Patrick's neck and cheeks grew warm, his body stiffened.

"Yeah, how 'ya been?" Thom, who was one of the track stars, ran his hand through his sandy, surfer boy hair, eking out a half-smile, an impossible dimple on each side.

Filmic squares of them smoking a joint in the parking lot with a druggy dream pop score invaded Patrick's mind. Cut to a basketball court, where they were shooting hoops, Patrick winning for a moment. Cut to the playroom in Thom's house, the lights low, Pink Floyd playing, the parents gone for the afternoon, nursing their Jack stolen from the liquor cabinet, them shoveling Doritos in their pieholes and pondering the mysteries of the String Theory.

"I'm doing okay" Patrick said. "Gawd, let me take this thing off. Come with me."

As they reached the hotel lobby, Patrick tugged once more at the zipper of his Wolverine head.

"There you are!" A waifish, blonde woman slinked up. "I'm Megan."

"Right, Megan, this is Patrick. An old buddy of mine," Thom said.

"Nice to meet you," Patrick said. He continued to wrestle with the zipper.

"It's stuck!" Patrick cried.

"What?"

The giant globe muffled Patrick's voice so he raised the volume. "IT'S STUCK!"

"Let me try." Thom jimmied the zipper. No luck. He pulled harder, causing Patrick to falter.

"Hey!" Patrick yelled. "Watch it."

"Sorry." Thom hands rested on Patrick's shoulders

"You gotta help me."

Thom turned to Megan. "Hey, listen, I need to help Patrick. Would you mind just hanging out here then head over to Flannigan's, you know, the bar down the street? This won't take long."

Megan smoothed her poured-on, pink dress. "Oh okay, no problem." She grabbed her shiny bag from a nearby table, gave Thom a peck on the cheek, and sashayed away.

Thom ushered Patrick across the parking lot and informed him about curbs and any upcoming obstacles. When they reached Thom's car, he opened the door and helped Patrick navigate the passenger's seat of his Smart Car. Patrick's fuzzy dome seemed to be a little too big for the space.

"You and your DUMB car," Patrick said.

"Ha! Funny as you ever were. Here..." Thom giggled as he guided Patrick's head, but it banged against the roof. "Tilt it a bit." Finally, he was in.

"What about my car?" Patrick said.

"I'll drive you back when we get that thing off of you."

"So...that Megan is a cute number."

"What? Can you speak up?"

"MEGAN! Are you WITH her?"

"Oh, please."

"Didn't think she was your type."

"What do you want me to say?"

"If you could see my face, you'd see I'm giving you an automatic eye roll."

The silence between them grew and was filled with the lonely putter of the small engine. As they drove along, Patrick's stomach churned and a bit of the pasta began to make its way up his esophagus. "Oh god, I'm gonna hurl."

"Oh, dear," Thom said.

Patrick detected a note of disdain in his voice. "What?"

"Nothing."

"My stomach really doesn't feel right." Patrick swallowed to suppress the sharp stomach juices that were gathering at the back of his throat. *I hope I don't throw up inside this thing.*

Thom slowed down, his headlights shining a few feet in front of the car, but just when it seemed he was home free, hit a pothole. Patrick jerked forward.

"Ugh! Man!"

"Sorry!" Thom grimaced. "Can you make it home?"

"Yes," Patrick whispered. "Please hurry."

#

As they inched into Patrick's apartment, Thom led the way. The walls were bare except for a few dusty photos. A large front window was lined with fluffy palms. Nearly every surface held a healthy, verdant plant. On his dining table was a spray of Gerbera daisies. Patrick rushed to his desk, tugged open a drawer that rattled a terra cotta pot full of ivy.

"Wow, it's a veritable jungle in here—" Thom said.

"Cut if off." Patrick handed him a pair of scissors.

"Really?"

"Really."

"You'll never be able to fix it."

"CUT it off." Patrick's throat tightened: more of the pasta rested at the back of his throat.

Thom placed the blades with surgical care at the base of the Wolverine skull. "Don't want to hit a jugular."

"You wouldn't care."

"What's that supposed to mean?"

"You know."

"No, I don't."

Patrick pivoted and drew close to Thom. "Let's get this thing off and we can talk."

"NO, I want to talk now. You're making me very uncomfortable."

"*You're* uncomfortable?" Patrick twisted the head. He tugged and turned it. Thom grabbed Patrick's hands, but they eluded him, seizing and fluttering like hummingbirds.

"STOP!" Thom said.

Patrick's fists flailed and curled into tight circles. Thom clutched Patrick's wrists and held them still. "Calm down."

"Get it off, for God's sake!"

As Thom snipped, the Wolverine's hair was slippery, unwieldy. He tried the zipper again, but it remained stubborn.

"Any luck?" Patrick's innards were cooking. His breath heated up his face and the head became an oven. Sweat poured from his hairline. Moisture pooled in his eyes. He placed both hands on the side of his noodle, pulled and yanked, tufts coming off in his hands.

"Aaaaah," Patrick roared. He tottered to a kitchen cabinet and returned with a hammer.

"Here."

"I can't do that. I could hurt you."

"You can. And WILL."

Patrick bent over the couch and braced himself. "Go ahead."

Thom whispered, "Be very still."

Patrick figured if he got a concussion, so be it. At least he wouldn't be imprisoned in hideousness anymore.

Thom slammed the hammer into the head. Nothing. He slammed harder. A small crack peeked through. He slammed again. The fissure expanded. Patrick dug his fingers into the hole and pulled—the material tore a smidge, but not enough.

"Do you have any cuticle scissors?" Thom said.

"I'm not a manicurist! Make the pair I gave you work."

Thom hesitated, then shoved the blades inside the furry mess.

"OUCH!" Patrick felt a small jab at the back of his neck.

Thom thrust his paw in the now-widened hole and *riiiip*, the head split in half. Patrick wrested himself from the offending object's suffocating grip. He threw it on the floor so hard it caused an end table to wobble. He began to choke, then went to the kitchen, and downed glass after glass of water.

"You okay?" Thom grasped Patrick's elbow.

"Sure." Patrick's face was glazed over with an icky film like plastic wrap and he stunk. He felt his stomach start to pretzel. "Be right back."

Patrick fled to his bathroom and inspected his face in the mirror: he was puffy and white, like he'd been filled with helium, not unlike the Pillsbury Dough Boy in the Macy's Thanksgiving Parade. He turned on the shower, gingerly stepped in and shivered. He tried to vomit, but somehow he couldn't. He pushed back the curtain, leaned out to pilfer through his medicine cabinet. *Tums! Yes! No, it's empty!* He hesitated, stuck his fingers down his throat and vomited. The shards of cheese pasta and crimson of his multiple Sea Breezes swirled towards the drain.

But then he saw them: skins of tomatoes. *So THAT was the red stuff in the pasta!* He was allergic to them, horribly so.

Even though his purging was warranted, and he was truly sick, he hadn't succumbed to forcing himself to vomit in a while. The fact that he'd made himself upchuck felt worse than the actual upchucking. Shame covered him like cream gravy. He assumed he was over his eating disorder, but perhaps it was still there. *That pasta was irresistible. Guess I need more therapy. But do I, really?*

Patrick gargled with mouthwash and emerged from the bathroom. He turned on the kitchen faucet and filled up his glass. He ran his tongue over his teeth. They were bumpy like pimples.

"You okay?" Thom leaned against the fireplace mantle and fiddled with his watch. "You were in there a long time."

"Yeah." Patrick exhaled. "Want something to drink? Ginger ale okay?"

He poured them each a glass and crept towards him, his water and the bubbly beverage threatening to spill.

Thom sipped the soda, then placed it on the fireplace mantle. "I owe you an apology."

"I trusted you."

"I led you on."

Patrick plunged his hands into his front pockets and peered into Thom's eyes. "I'll never get over Alison walking in, the look on her face when she saw me walking out of the bathroom without my pants, and you all buck naked sprawled out on the sofa. I suspect she started the scuttlebutt, though she swore she wouldn't tell anyone. Did you see her tonight? I swear she was on my heels and I couldn't seem to ditch her."

"No, didn't see her."

"Can't believe she had the gall to talk to me. She never apologized."

"Actually, everything, the whole snafu, was my fault. I left the playroom door unlocked."

"It was my fault because I loved you." There they were, those three naked words. They circled in the ether.

"I did care about you."

"Care is for puppies."

Thom gazed out the window. "I'm sorry, I just didn't know who I was then. Maybe it was a phase."

"Are you still in the phase? What, with Megan?"

"I'd be disowned." Thom's face greyed.

"You're safe with me."

"We connected. All our inside jokes. You got me."

"And you got *me*." Patrick shifted closer.

Thom tipped his head down and brushed the carpet with his toe.

"Spray painting, barely evading the cops, and running over that stop sign."

"Guilty! I didn't know how to drive a stick shift. I told you that."

"I know, I know." Thom's mouth formed a tender gasp Patrick knew well. "We had some good times."

"We did." Patrick leaned in, their lips met, and his pulse quickened. He unswaddled a familiar, ragged part of himself, a place that he thought was forever lost. The glue was there. It was as if they'd never parted.

Thom lingered, then pulled away. His eyes found the floor. The silence was thick.

Patrick stroked the back of his neck and massaged the place where the scissor had nicked him, then examined his fingers. "No blood. Guess I'll be okay."

"Do you still have that thing where you purge?"

"Mostly no." Patrick stirred. "But I did throw up in there because I ate tomatoes."

"Oh, gosh."

"I feel better now. You were the first person who knew about me, what I did."

"I always thought you looked great. You didn't need to lose weight. You look pretty fit."

"Thanks, I try." Patrick's skin prickled, as if it had been stripped away.

Thom picked up the two half-shells of the Wolverine head. He examined them as if they were precious, ancient artifacts. "Really did a number on this."

"You can have that. It'll be your souvenir."

"Right." Thom placed the broken halves together. "Maybe it can be repaired?"

"I've got a better idea." Patrick retreated to the kitchen and returned with a dark green Hefty bag. "Toss that thing in here."

"Cradled"

Sheila often thought about walking out to her mailbox naked. Would the neighbors call the cops? Would someone throw rotten tomatoes? Would anyone even care?

Instead, she wrapped her robe around her ample body and began her trek. No mail. Hadn't come yet. *I'm invisible.*

Despite her applaudable pluck, her life was a study in being unseen. Picked last for Red Rover. Sat alone during lunch. Left in front of the middle school waiting for her mom to arrive, long after everyone had grown up and died. Then there was the teasing: *Miss Piggy. Tub 'o Lard. Fatty McFat Pants.*

Bob, her husband, watched from the upstairs guest room, his office. Lately, he'd been distant, absorbed in his work. She peered up into the windows. His profile, unflinching, was as still as a brick.

Five weeks ago, she had a hysterectomy. Fibroids and hyperplasia. Time for her old rusty uterus to go. However, she was on the mend, almost back to normal, whatever that was.

When she informed her husband she needed the operation, he blinked, his eyes filling with inky darkness, a smoothed-over indifference. "How much will that cost, after insurance?"

No, *I'm so sorry.* No, *you must be scared.* Instead, "Do you mind making more coffee?"

"I'm going out," Sheila announced in the doorway of his office. "Do we need anything from the store?"

"Let's see." Bob ran his hand through his ancient, grey hair. "I could use some cereal."

Sheila changed clothes and drove to the store in a Honda that had been a consolation prize for losing a primo job she'd had as head of marketing for a medical equipment company. The car ran better than she did—smooth, quiet.

Sailing along, thoughts of Hal curled into her frontal lobe, the place where maturity was supposed to have congealed. She lived for the adolescent thrill of romance, believed that a concentric circle of frenzy could exist between two people for time eternal. That's what she felt when she met Hal at yoga last year. Something ineffable from him garroted her.

Now, a "For Rent" sign hung in the yoga center's window, and Hal and his wife moved to another state. Hal's wife knew—and so did Bob. After therapy, he claimed to forgive Sheila, but she could see his lingering resentment like an aura. It inched up between them, rustling the whisper-thin box that housed the tableau of their lives.

She circled the block a few times, then on to a nearby convenience store, where she grabbed an over-priced box of Cheerios. Her husband would be miffed, but he'd never say so.

Back home, she slapped the cereal on a pantry shelf and then put on her Boot Camp DVD. She needed to slim down, tried for decades. Lying in the hospital, and recouping for six weeks had given her plenty of time to think about her broken and bloated body. She remembered 10 years ago, when she met Bob on a blind date and how she lost weight with Weight Watchers. When they'd decided to marry, they were both pushing 40. Marriage felt like the right thing to do.

Sheila shed her black leggings and oversized t-shirt. Her corpus was a war zone, pocked and puckered, a forgotten hinterland. She pawed her sallow face, smoothed the bags under her eyes, then placed her palms on her checks and pulled, creating the illusion of a facelift. She slipped into her tight, bulge-revealing workout gear and headed to her office. She rolled her desk chair out of the way and pressed "Play."

When the DVD began, the music was peppier than she'd remembered: a pulsing synth track, booming base and shrill electric guitars. As the young, svelte blonde spokes-actress instructor bark-purred out the moves, Sheila gave it her all. Streeeetch, kick, streeeeetch, kick, burpee! She hit the floor, pain shotgunning through her body, then stumbled. Sweat pooled under her arms and breasts. *I can do this. I am not old!*

Halfway through, she stopped for a water break and heard a knock on her door.

"Hi, I have a Zoom meeting starting in a few. Can you please turn it down?" Bob's shoulders seemed extra slumped, his body the shape of a question mark.

"Sure," said Sheila, noticing his flat eyes as he closed the door. "Anything for you, dear."

She turned down the volume, began again, jumping higher, stretching longer and harder, trying to exercise her way back into her youth, her salad days, during which, she hated salads. She stopped, her breath ragged, and caught her reflection in a mirror. She studied her wild, irregular landscape. Her hands found her folds and kneaded them. *I can't escape my flesh.*

"Aaaaah." Sheila's stomach wambled. The stabs arrived in succession. *I'm dying, please make it stop.* Her head muzzy, she grabbed her pelvis and felt something wet between her thighs: her fingers were covered in blood. She ran to the bathroom, stripped naked, and grabbed toilet paper. The bleeding was relentless.

"BOB! HELP!"

She bounded up the stairs, blood waterfalling down her leg, and burst into his room. On his laptop screen was a checkerboard of faces. Tiny mouths opened. Jaws dropped. Murmurings commenced. Heads jiggled in spasms like minnows darting just under the water's surface.

"What the—?" Bob scrambled to turn off Zoom.

"Help!" Sheila clutched her abdomen, jackknifed, and fell.

"Oh, god." Bob slammed his computer shut. "What did you do? I've warned you about overdoing it."

Sheila collapsed into a mess of tears. She buried her head in his sweatshirt. His pine aftershave filled her nostrils. The scent was from another time, when there was electricity between them, when passion took shape around them, when they tried to conceive, but after five miscarriages, they gave up.

"They saw me," Sheila said, her eyes wide, urgent, lost in a weave of fresh truth.

"No they didn't." Bob cradled her as he thumbed 911. "But I'm here. I see you."

"Paradise"

I'd been on matchmaker.com for about six months. *Snatchmaker,* I called it. Everyone I knew on this site was gettin' a little action. It was also where some of my friends had met their husbands. *Husbands.* Hell, I've had three. Billy, I left him. Dustin, he died. Then Jake. He and I worked together in the ER, but another nurse busted us up. The bitch.

Jesse's photo came up. He had a mop of dusty blond hair with an irresistible cowlick. I wanted to wet my fingers, reach in the picture and smooth it down. I looked into his blue-jean colored eyes, sweet eyes that were all sparkly, eager and needy, and decided I wanted to know him. We made a plan to meet at The Grapevine.

The Grapevine was a little stone cottage, a dump really, with a splintered wooden front door that always looked like it had been given a fresh coat of red paint. Inside, there were mirrors and neon flashing signs that said Budweiser, Coors, and Colt 45. They blinked and winked at you. The music, usually Stones, burst from an old school jukebox and often, the bone-shaking bass could curl your eyelids. The air was an intoxicating blend of cigarettes and beer, a comforting aroma that told me I was home and yet the cracked, aging walls were strange, the tributaries seemed to possess dark secrets. If you got down to it, it was a place where anything goes, a magnet for the motley. Like walking into a garage sale where you'd see a juicer, a pair of shorts, and a wig on the same table. There was Wayne with long, stringy Crisco hair who wore mini-skirts and nuzzled the neck of his preppy, blonde girlfriend. Loud-talking, downtown lawyers with loosened ties and sweaty brows. Hipsters in jaunty berets and head-to-toe black who smoked those stubby, French cigarettes, their eyes half-mast. The wine was not crap—it was a damn miracle. People came here for a salve, a balm, but not like the one in Gilead.

I worked in the ER as a trauma nurse. Sometimes I got a little blow at The Grapevine if I was lucky. Not that I couldn't get Demerol, Xanax, and other smack from a doctor pal of mine who wrote me scripts. But I was trying to stop.

Every day I saw all kinds of things that kept me up at night. Images I couldn't shake.

Stabs in the neck.

Hands hanging off by the tendons.

Icepicks in the eyes.

They said you'd get used to it. Grow a shell. I'd wanted to answer my call. To be of service, help people, fix the world. Wanted my pituitary case to matter when I was six feet under. What had stuck with me since I was little was a story about Mother Teresa. She was over there in India helping the lepers and then someone came into her colony who wanted to assist. Story goes that this aid worker person was so overwhelmed with all the suffering—there were hundreds of them—that he said they couldn't possibly help all the people, to which Mother Teresa replied, "You can't help *all* the people. You help *one person* at a time."

I needed fixing, too. Truth was, I was on Snatchmaker looking for sweet bodies to press against mine, to help me forget. I missed that almost-suffocating feeling of falling asleep tangled up in a man's arms. I had a soul ache, a spiritual migraine. Some days it hurt just to get out of bed. At 18, I'd been a prom queen but now, at 39, I covered my grey with Lady Clairol blonde and didn't dare leave the house without base makeup, undereye concealer, and lipstick.

I coaxed my next-door neighbor, Kurt, to go with me to The Grapevine to meet Jesse. Kurt had a thin grey goatee and liked men. He and I were relationship twins, bookends, each with buckets of kill-you tales of heartbreak, each holding torches for exes who could never love us back. I pulled on my short skirt, slipped on my pink fuzzy sweater, fluffed my hair, and spritzed some perfume. Kurt was waiting by my car, his arms folded, his face in his phone. "Here she comes."

I opened the flimsy, scarlet door of The Grapevine, Kurt on my heels, and inched past the six-foot six bouncer, who was wearing a CBGB t-shirt that didn't quite cover his big stomach and black gauges the size of checkers in both ears. Smoke hung in the air like a curse. Along one wall, a few people sat in dilapidated armchairs and a gash in the shade of a lamp cut a razor through the darkness. A '70s heavy metal song was playing, the backbeat rumbled up my legs. I passed a thicket of heads, arms, and legs, which expanded and contracted like a lung.

I headed to the back room to the pool table. Above it hung an ugly gold and red lamp, the dust motes swirling. All the regulars were there. Kurt ordered a whiskey. As usual, I had a few buttery chardonnays made by Francis Ford Coppola. I always imagined that Mr. Francis would pop up from behind the bar and whisk me away to Hollywood. Instead, there was Cletis, the bartender, who had an Amish beard and was missing a middle finger. When he shot me the bird, lovingly of course, he'd say, "Read between the lines, sister."

I felt a hand on my waist, but pushed it away. "You better be Jesse," I said. It was. He looked a bit like his picture, only older and more faded. He had a crooked smile. His eyes weren't plain old blue, they were sudden, azure. His hair had grown and sweat had taped a mush-colored swatch of it to his forehead. He had on a red and blue flannel shirt with those snap buttons. A little chest hair peeked out at me from the top of the second button, the tease. He smelled good, but I caught a whiff of something weird. Maybe he'd gargled with Listerine.

"You look just like your pretty picture." Jesse wiggled his eyebrows. I blushed and pretended I was more embarrassed than I was.

We slammed together, talking, interrupting, and congealing like fast, rudderless friends. Our shared interests wrapped their tentacles around us. We were drunk on the things we held in common. We saw our future in an instant.

I like square dancing, TOO.

You have a motorcycle? My dad LOVED his motorcycles!

Really? MY great uncle was a fireman!

You were NOT born with a toe on the bottom of your foot! My brother has a third nipple!

Words stopped. I stroked the soft hair on his forearm. "You look like Brad Pitt."

"Takeoff those wine goggles, woman." He kissed me square on the mouth. "Let's play some pool."

Jesse beat me, fair and square. I could never get that pole to slide between my thumb and forefinger. He got all fancy, putting the stick behind his back, breaking the balls in a big, noisy explosion. Kurt stood by and applauded with slow, irritating claps.

A guy with a face like a mouse, whiskers and all, with little round glasses sat down on the torn black leather booths that lined the room. The more I looked at this new guy, the more he reminded me of Stuart Little, that movie rat. The delicate bones of his face bugged me. He was an ill-preserved man, thin with a bad haircut. I suspected he ate a bad diet. His shirt was one of those that you wore if you worked at a gas station. "Jim" was stitched on the pocket.

"Got a light? Jim said.

"Sure," I said. But before I could get my lighter out of my purse, Kurt lunged in with his. The flame shot up all tall and prideful.

"Jim Dandy, I take it," Kurt said.

Jim leaned into Kurt, crossed his legs like a lady and inhaled. But he sucked in so hard you could see the outline of his skull, then he exhaled a long, obnoxious puff. "Dandy or Randy. You decide."

Kurt took a seat next to Jim Dandy, looked him up and down, gave him his requisite head-to-toe sweep.

"Kurt. Jim. Jim, Kurt," I said. "Just want to make sure everyone knows everyone." They nodded.

Then I broke the pool balls with a cackle, but they barely moved, except for one red ball that drifted to the side of the table.

"Honey, let me help you," Jesse said. He bent his long, drink-of-water body over the table, his jeans taut against his thighs, his hair hanging, shaggy over his eyes. He grinned, exposing a dimple, and while not taking his eyes off of me, hit the 8-ball in the side pocket, clean and clear.

"There you go."

"So I see." My nether parts started to thrum. The TV in the corner up near the ceiling was playing old MTV. The Thompson Twins sang, "Hold Me Now." I sang along, serenading the fumes around me, hoping to catch Jesse's gaze, but he was in a zone.

I leaned up next to the table, just as he was about to play. "You're a pro."

"Oh, go on," Jesse said, pointing his cue at an orange ball, but this time his hip was hiked up on the edge of the table, his elbow at a 45-degree angle.

"I mean, that last shot. You didn't even look at the table."

"You mean, like this?" Crack! The orange ball in the side pocket, his eyes locked in on mine.

This is starting to get good.

I gulped my wine, throwing my head back with high drama, running my fingers through my hair. I ordered another, downed that one, then went over to the other side of the room, where Kurt and Jim Dandy were chatting it up.

"You all doing okay?" I said.

"Never better," Kurt said. He reached over and rested his hand on Jim's knee, but Jim never gave him a look.

After the fourth game, Jesse had swamped me every time. He laid his cue against the wall.

"I'm getting tired of this place. It's loud," Jesse said. "A friend is having a moving out party. I'll pick up a couple six-packs. Here's the address, honey." His eyes were suddenly translucent and staring me down. "You and your buddy wanna come with?"

I was in.

Jim Dandy nodded twice with force, pulled himself up, exchanged whispers with Jesse, then slogged towards the door. Kurt and I followed, and got in my Impala, my trashcan-on-wheels.

"You hitting on Jim?" I said, as we pulled from the curb.

"What?" Kurt mumbled, his eyes closed. His lips parted as if he was about to speak. His stomach pooched out over his belt. I was surprised because we had both gotten these Tummy Tuck Belts from QVC and had gone to Jazzercise religiously and at one point, he'd actually lost his beer gut, but no more. I was betting he was back eating those Little Debbie's.

"You had your hand on that guy Jim's knee," I said. "Be careful. I don't need you getting a disease or murdered."

"I'll be good. I've got an early morning."

"So do I. Got in a mess of trouble last time I was late."

#

As Kurt and I pulled up in front of the house, a line of people filed in, streaming underneath the porch light. The place was not special. Slatted with slouching shutters. Typical for this neighborhood. 1950s houses that people were either demolishing and putting up McMansions, or fixing them up to be cute and overpriced with seasonal flags out front flapping in the wind all smug and self-important.

"You ready?" I said.

"Indeed," Kurt grunted.

As we made our way up the front walk, fireflies pulsed over a pitiful, balding lawn, where a tattered couch sat with part of the guts spilling out like it has just vomited. On it was a girl with long legs crossed who was perched on the lap of a large, muscled guy wearing a gimme cap. Her skirt was so short that, if it was daylight, you might see pay dirt. The tip of her cigarette glowed like the red planet.

I saw Jesse in the doorway. "Hey you." He took me by the hand and led me inside.

The walls were stripped. Patches of sheet rock glared at us. In a few spots, wallpaper hung its head, curling. In the living room, there was another couch, this one plaid, beside a few folding chairs and a broken-down baby blue Lay-Z-Boy, all huddled together as if a meeting had just ended. A TV was playing, but no one was watching. The room was awash with paper plates, empty Chinese food cartons, Budweiser cartons, red Solo Cups. People were writing on the walls. One guy was drawing a sunflower with an evil grin. Another girl was sketching what looked like her self-portrait. A large shirtless guy in overalls who had man boobs sat on a lone paint can like a circus clown on a tiny bicycle.

"Here," Jesse said, handing me a marker and pulling me over to an empty space of wall, away from the crowd.

"Get going," Jesse said. "Show me what 'cha got."

"I can't draw."

"Write something then."

"Okay, I'll write a story."

"More like it."

"It's a tragedy. Full of blood and shit," I said. "Swimming pools. Movie stars."

But then my tale evaporated. That extra chardonnay I'd chugged at the bar kicked in with blunt force. All I could do was doodle. Every stroke was a burden.

Then Jesse crumpled to the floor.

"Dear God," I said. I helped him stagger over to the couch and the people who were on it hopped up real fast, heads turning with furrowed brows, mumbling concern.

"I'm a nurse," I said, struck sober.

I laid him down like a corpse on a lumpy mess of empty beer cans and dirty throw pillows. I felt his wrist. He had a pulse. I'd seen many a guy like him brought into the ER after a bender, passed out, but he'd be okay. He was just drunk. Besides, I was used to men cutting out unexpectedly.

"Wake up, honey." I gave him a pat on each cheek. Smoothed his hair.

Until this point, I had been able to erase the memory of a homeless man in the ER that died in my arms the other night. But now his ragged face was everywhere I looked.

After a few minutes, I tapped Jesse's cheeks and he stirred.

"Whoa," Jesse said. "What'd I miss?"

"Me."

Jesse's sleepy, soft mouth struggled to smile.

Jim Dandy had the remote and started changing the channels on the TV. *I Love Lucy*. Monster trucks. Richard Simmons exercise show.

"Who lives here anyway?" Kurt said.

"I don't know and I don't care just as long as the beer keeps flowing," Jim Dandy said.

Kurt had his arm around Jim Dandy and they had lodged themselves next to Jesse, who rested his head on my lap. There we were. The Four Stooges: Kurt, Jim Dandy, Jesse and me.

Suddenly, an 80-pound golden Labrador jumped up on the couch, dropped a slobbery tennis ball and sniffed Jesse's crotch.

"Go on, now!" Jesse said, and threw the ball across the room. It hit a skinny girl with a Marine cut. She threw it back, gave the girl next to her a quick peck on the cheek, then continued to scribble on the wall. More people milled in and out of the room, tennis-shoed guys spilled drinks, cutesy girls in wedges tripped over carpet scraps and squealed. A few lonely, bearded dudes drifted by and bumped into the walls.

My back started hurting bad, like real bad, so I laid down on the floor and watched the gooey ball in the distance bounce across the crusty carpet, which smelled like a dumpster. Cheetos. Gum wrappers. Cigarette butts.

"Gonna hit the head," Kurt said, and disappeared into the back of the house, leaving Jim Dandy slumped over on a pillow holding his drink.

"Don't be gone long," I said. Kurt was a pretty good wingman. He and I had a history of late-night tearful phone calls and many episodes of pouring our hearts out into our wine glasses near closing time. But tonight I wasn't sure if bringing him along was a good idea.

The lab returned with the gooey ball, his big toenaily paws trampled my head. Jim Dandy jumped up and threw the ball, then fell back down on the couch, his thin lips suckling his beer. I raised up on my elbows at the same time that Jesse extended his hand to me.

"Hey, why don't you get back up and visit with me?"

I rose with effort, my body defying me, but as I sat down, Jim Dandy scooted to the other side of Jesse.

"What is it that you do?" I asked Jesse. I knew, but I wanted to hear him say it. It was on his Snatchmaker profile.

"I am a sandwich stylist at Subway," Jesse said.

"I don't think so," I said.

Jesse stiffened, then he pushed his forehead clean up to his hairline. "Yes, I am."

"No, you're Brad Pitt's body double," I said.

Jesse's posture changed, his whole body, a warm smile, and he flicked me on the nose with his forefinger. "Fresh," he said.

"Fresh! Just like Subway sandwiches," Jim Dandy said.

"I, myself, am partial to the pickles," I said.

Jesse smirked and cut me a look. I wished Jim would leave me and Jesse alone. And where was Kurt? I was about to say something ugly, I didn't know what, to Jim Dandy to make him go away (of course, later I'd blame my rudeness on being drunk), but then he reached in his pocket and pulled out some pills, Xanax.

"Party favors," Jim Dandy said. He popped one in his mouth and washed it down with his beer. He handed me one, then Jesse. We regarded the tiny promises of happiness in our hands. Jesse's skin glistened and he seemed to look through me, into my sinews. Then as we if were at communion, we palmed them into our mouths.

#

4 a.m. As I awoke, the couch was moving. The overhead light was out and the room was deserted, a liquor bottle wasteland. The movement was coming from Jesse beside me. He and Jim Dandy were kissing. I squenched my eyes shut, then opened them. It was still happening. I wasn't dreaming.

"Hey, you two!" I hit Jesse's thigh with my fist and they stopped. Their mouths parted.

"Jealous?" Jim Dandy said.

I jumped up. I had to escape. Men usually cheated on me with women.

Now men? My gut contracted. I'd been sucker-punched and I started weeping, nothing made sense.

Jesse grabbed my arm, and pulled me close. His breath was a beer factory. When Jim Dandy saw us, his eyes opened like he had just been goosed, and with an air of clean indifference, he said, "I'm outta here."

"Me, too," I said. "I thought you liked me."

"I do, honey."

"You have a funny way of showing it."

I was a hypocrite. Once I'd gotten drunk and made out with a woman I didn't know. Jesse loosened his grip and held my cheek in his palm.

"You're beautiful, you know that?"

A blue flame of desire ricocheted up my spine. Jesse's lips parted, he cocked his head, then pulled my face closer to his. He assumed an inhuman angle, lurching forward, a smoothed over awkwardness. Billy, my first husband, used to pinch my cheeks between his thumb and third finger and shout into my face, my heart watching, my brain burning. But Jesse's voice was soft, repentant, angelic. His hand cupped my face and seemed to hold the meaning of life.

"Do you forgive me?" Jesse said.

"Sure."

We kissed. He fondled my breast, trying to be sensual, but it felt like he was giving me an exam. "Too many thumbs," I said. "It tickles."

Jesse giggled. "I want it to."

"Where's Kurt?" I said.

By this time, I was worried. It would kill me if something happened to him.

"He never came back after he went to pee. Think he might have driven your car home. He was fishing around in your purse for the keys at one point."

Kurt took my car? Seriously? Perhaps he felt he needed to, but I was still pissed. However, my anger was unreachable, lodged somewhere between clouded layers of confusion and booze—and that pill.

"I need to go home. Gonna call an Uber."

"I can take you."

"No, I'm fine."

"Come on," he said, his lips pink with hope. "I don't want the night to end. But I have to make a stop first."

We stumbled into Jesse's El Camino. I unzipped my skirt to stop the digging into my stomach. Alright, I was a little overweight. Okay, 50 pounds. I called it *life*. If you carved into my body with a knife, you'd see the memories, the pain, the everything. Jesse lit a cigarette and rolled down the window as we pulled away from the curb. I thought I was going to get sick, but I swallowed my saliva. The seats were cold on my thighs and I shivered. The sun's soft, slivery fingers of near morning reaching up from the horizon caused a glare and I flipped the visor down.

We drove along and passed some nice houses with gates, big lawns and green, trimmed hedges. I wondered about all the rich people inside, what their problems were. Then the houses got smaller and closer together.

"Shady Grove Funeral Home?" I said, as he slowed down. He eased his car to a gentle stop in front. I followed him up to a grey house with a wrap-around porch.

"I need to use the restroom," I said. "What are we doing here?"

"You'll see."

Jesse's eyes caught mine, but they had changed: they were marbles, not real human eyes. But I wasn't scared. I'd seen worse.

"I'm gonna go right here if we don't get inside."

"Hang on."

Jesse got out a mess of jangly keys from his pocket and then we were in. The lone bulb hanging overhead gave off a harsh, grey light and caused me to notice his jagged, shocked teeth I hadn't seen earlier. I raced in as fast as I could on my too-tall high heels, but I didn't know where I was going.

"Down the hall, then turn right." Jesse's laughter rippled behind me.

I ran to the bathroom, but it was too late. Warm urine ran down my thighs. The bitter smell filled my nostrils. I wiped my legs and thighs with soapy, thin paper towel, which was cold and clammy. I got a glimpse of my face in the mirror. Mascara was having a party around my eyes. I didn't try to fix it. But I did put on lipstick. I was fond of looking at my tube of Chanel lipstick I got at Neiman-Marcus. The brand legitimized me. Made me feel like I mattered. My last husband, Jake the cheater, didn't mind when I kissed him and got red all over his face. He looked like a child wearing face paint at a church carnival. As my bladder cleared I realized Jesse had keys to this place. What did that mean?

His voice rang out from another room, but I was not sure where. As I rounded the corner, I entered a large room that smelled of God-knows-what, chemicals, and I became instantly woozy. I steadied myself in the door frame and then I saw them: six gurneys with cadavers under sheets that were arranged in neat rows and reminded me of twin beds at summer camp. Cabinets and refrigerators lined the jaundiced walls. A few posters that detailed human anatomy hung in rows. People had died in my arms, but I'd never seen where they went after they were taken away.

"Welcome to paradise," Jesse said. He was hunched over by a cabinet and had a tray in front of him. He was rolling up a dollar bill. On the counter sat a big bag of coke. Sugary and proud.

"So, this is your job?"

Jesse didn't look at me, but addressed the countertop. "I didn't want to tell you the truth. Thought you might run."

"I would have."

"It was my daddy's business." He turned, showing me a cookie sheet of white lines, then carried it over like he was Jeeves the butler and with a flourish, set it on the counter in front of me.

"Help yourself."

"No, you first."

"This is Peruvian." After Jesse took one long inhale, I grabbed his rolled bill. I couldn't resist. A hole of want folded in on me. I was a flesh-and-bones mistake.

Again and again, my nose was up on those snowy skid marks. *Numbskull. Numb nuts. Numb nose.* I had tasted the pearly nectar. I was flying, immortal.

"Actually," he said. "I've got a better idea."

He threw back a sheet on a stretcher. What I saw made my heart quiver: the most beautiful boy I'd ever seen. With a gunshot in the right temple. Jesse was cute, but this guy, *this guy.*

The dead man's skin was olive. Perhaps he was Italian. His eyes were closed and beaded with thick, lush eyelashes. His brows were two ebony inchworms. He had a tattoo of a cross on his right bicep. His legs were muscular, luxurious, and long. His penis was curled in a "J" and looked like it was taking a nap. I touched his lips with two fingers; they were swollen, cold, discolored. His form made the room shimmer; the fluorescent lights shed a movie-star glow on him. I'd helped people live again when we pressed those clappers to lifeless chests. I'd seen the pulse of life leaping back into their still bodies. But now, the aching stillness of this man screamed before me.

"Suicide," Jesse said. "Haven't fixed him up yet."

"Embalmed," I choked out.

Jesse began to sway, then grabbed the bag of coke, removed a miniature spoon from a drawer, dipped it into the white powder, and delicately like he was sprinkling salt on his tater tots, made a straight line on the chest of the dead man.

"Here we go," Jesse said. Delirium carved up his face.

"This is wrong," I said. "WRONG! "

"I know. But I don't think he'd mind."

Then he sniffed the coke right off the body. Jesse jumped back. Did the pogo. His boots slammed on the floor. Then he began a slow, girly snicker that escalated into a maniacal shriek.

"Stop it, stop it right now." I yanked his arm, but he escaped my grip, pushing me away. I looked into his eyes. They glowed. My life was radiating chaos and this was the fiery center.

I might have been twisted. I might have done some bad things in my life: mooning my ex when he was on a picnic with his mother, shoplifting makeup, peeing in the parking lot after a ZZ Top concert, wishing instant death and fatal diseases on people who had wronged me, fingering a knife at dinner after my last husband told me he was leaving me, imagining plunging it into his temple. But I'd never hovered this close to savagery.

As Jesse wound down his dancing, the shiny devices, knives and scalpels, that in the ER were part of life, seemed to rise up in front of me. Fear scissored through me. My veins pressed against my skin. While I didn't really think of myself as an addict, I'd heard they had to hit rock bottom before they could recover. A voice inside asked if I'd just hit mine. Because if this wasn't it, how much further down did I need to go?

Then, as if from another dimension, somewhere outside of me, I was able to shake myself back. I grabbed my purse, burst through the doors, stumbled down the stairs, and staggered onto the street. Some people find their calling, love their jobs and live happily ever after. Jesse's happily ever after was milking his mad crush on death. I, on the other hand, had warred against it, trying to save lives. But I was done. My skin was too thin. The suffering I'd endured had whittled it away, exposing the walking nerve ending that I was, had always been.

As I floated along, there was a loud hum of silence that insisted on being heard. In the emptiness, the world buzzed.

"Josie's Documented Evidence"

She wore blue smocks. Smoked long, brown More cigarettes. Looked like a slightly taller Linda Hunt. And frequently when I passed by her station was talking about *documented evidence.*

What kind of evidence exactly? That if one of the too-hot-to-touch, ancient hair dryers was left on too long it would explode and burn up the salon? That the new shampoo girl was robbing the coke machine? That the end papers for the permanent wave gel were too thin and disintegrating in Mrs. Grayden's hair?

Who could say?

Josie was one of my dad's stylists, or operators, at Curly's, his salon. And she was operating in her own sense of reality.

Every time anyone walked by, she was theorizing about something. My brother, though, had the inside story.

He said she told him that in the height of people being bitten by sharks in Florida that she had "documented evidence" that people were being bitten by sharks up and down the Texas coast. And if we valued our lives, we should steer clear of this death trap.

"I am not goin' there! No way. No how. You won't catch me there. Bud and I'll just take our trailer somewhere else, somewhere safe!"

My brother also told me that he had heard that Josie's dire need for "documented evidence" stemmed from her childhood. When she was 10 years old, she told her family that a raccoon would visit her at night and cling to her window screen. No one believed her. They thought it was a cat—her dad always said she had an "overactive imagination," until a local newspaper ran an article about a rash of raccoons hitting attics and basements in town. From that point on, she vowed to record data—definitive proof—in any way she could.

One day, my dad got ill. His usual sub at the salon was Houston, but he was chock-a-block busy. So Josie stepped up and stepped in to take care of my dad's customers—one of whom was coming in to get her hair fixed for the Symphony Ball.

Let's call her Madge.

Her family fortune was from the Pig Pens. They served up the finest pork barbecue in the Southwest. Made big money from this. Rumor had it that their children were all vegans, so you know that stirred up some heated family conversations.

"You know what ruined the Pig Pens? Aaaair-conditioning!" Madge said over and over. "Aaaaair-conditioning!" as if this modern convenience had the audacity to do her this wrong.

My dad had a certain way of dealing with his upper-end clientele. He spoke of the latest charity events and kept up with the social pages in the paper religiously. He could also speak very knowledgeably about opera and literature. On the other hand, Josie's idea of culture was more NASCAR on a Saturday with a Big Gulp.

Nevertheless, Madge was coming in. And Josie was going to do her hair.

Here's the story as I know it.

Madge arrived in a navy St. John's knit suit and walked with a rickety cane. Her thin, in-need-of-coloring, brown-grey hair was in a state of disarray, windswept, as if she'd just gotten off the Tilt-O-Whirl at the Texas State Fair.

She was also a fashion icon, at every gala and always got her photo in the society pages of the Dallas newspaper. She usually brought her purse-sized dog, Bubbles, with her to the salon, but not today. He was at the hairdresser himself.

As she approached the reception desk and inquired about my dad, suddenly, her voice became elevated. Hushed murmurs turned into audibly upset tones.

"Well! That just won't do! I want John to do my hair. He's the only one who I can trust," she said, tapping her cane forcefully with every syllable.

Josie saw this, and approached with caution.

"Madge, I know you must be disappointed, but I assure you I can do just as good a job as John. If you come right with me we can get started." And away they went.

Josie grabbed some towels to make a soft pillow, upon which Madge would lay her head for her shampoo. Madge ambled up, negotiated the chair with lots of frowns and tisks, then plopped herself down with a heave-ho. The cane rattled to the floor.

"Don't worry, I'll get that," Josie said.

A burst of water came out of the sprayer and onto Madge's fluffy, shock of hair.

"OOOOH that is TOO COLD! Could you turn on some hot water, for Pete's sake?"

"Madge, this water is 75 degrees, which is not cold, but I can make it hotter." Josie turned up the hot water.

"This water is still COLD! Lord Sakes, I'm 'bout to freeze to death!"

Josie turned the knob once more. "Is that better? I hope so. I have documented evidence that this water is, in fact, now 85 degrees."

"I suppose, but that first blast was bad. I'm just used to John's shampoos."

Josie rinsed her hair, then wrapped a towel around her head like a swami.

They made their way to Josie's chair, Madge teetering like a bowling pin every step of the way.

As Madge sat down, Josie cut to the chase. "So are we doing the usual today? Roll up and comb out?"

Madge eked out a stern, "Yes, indeed."

Josie began combing Madge's hair, which was a thick, tangled spidery web.

"So how's business? Your grandkids? Been on any exotic trips lately?"

Madge grimaced. "Can you comb a little more gently? I am tender headed."

"Of course, my apologies. You've got lots of hair."

"If you wouldn't comb so fast it wouldn't tug at my scalp. John knows my head."

"You know, I am as sorry as I can be, but I have to admit that I try to work with what God brings my way," Josie said. "Goobers or Raisinettes? I've got both."

"Just hand me the Goobers." Madge snarled.

Soon Madge's head was a beacon of hot pink, hard curlers the size of a world globe.

"Okay, let's put you under the dryer, get you cookin' good lookin'."

"Well, it's about time."

Madge steadied herself, grabbed her cane, then hooked her arm square-dance style into Josie's arm and off they went to the dryer.

Josie gingerly sat her down, careful to make sure her head was properly positioned under the plastic dome. She set the timer for an hour so her hair would be set to perfection. As much of a pain in the rump roast she was, Josie did care for the woman and understood that she was old and her legs probably hurt.

"Can I get you anything else, Madge?"

"What?" Madge said, in a loud, opera voice. The dryers were noisy and obscured Josie's voice.

"CAN I GET YOU ANYTHING ELSE? A COKE COLA? DR. PEPPER? HOT COFFEE?"

"Do you have any crudité?"

"Come again?"

"CRU-DI-TAY."

"Uh, sure." Josie cocked her head to one side, then bent down again.

"What is Crew-di ... what is that exactly? I don't know that drink."

Madge pulled up the dryer hood and spoke with clipped syllables into Josie's face with all the kindness she could muster.

"John usually has these little snacky things, chopped up veggies, you know, carrots and celery, which are commonly referred to as 'crudité'—it's a French word—so I was wondering if there were any to be had."

"Oh! Those! If you had spoken a language I understood, I would have made the connection. Let me go find them. Anything else you need?"

"I'd be pleased as punch if you could get me a fashion magazine, a Vogue." Madge lowered the hood over her head.

"Okay, let me look."

Josie got the crudité from the fridge, then rummaged around on the magazine rack, and made her way back to Madge. She approached slowly, looking down like a child about to be disciplined.

"I'm sorry, Madge. All I found was a *Ladies Home Journal* and a *Cosmo*. No *Vogue*," Josie said. "And here's your crew cuts."

"Thank you," Madge said, relieved to see the life-giving morsels. "And I'll take the *Cosmo*. Catch up on my sex tips."

An hour passed and it was time for Josie to fetch Madge. Josie put out her fifth More cigarette of the day, and scurried out of the smoking room to get Madge.

"That dryer was scalding hot," Madge said, as she sat down in Josie's chair.

"Honey, next time holler. How can I help you if you don't tell me anything?"

"You should have checked on me instead of standing in the back smoking your cancer sticks."

"You know, you are right. I am so sorry. I am a very bad person."

"For goodness sakes, Josie, don't talk like that."

Silence hung heavy in the air like a mushroom cloud.

Josie brushed, and combed. Combed and brushed. Teased and then backcombed until Madge's hair was a masterpiece.

"There you go. Done as toast," Josie said. "All we need to do is spray you, then I can call your driver."

"All righty then."

Josie retrieved her Aqua Net and gave Madge's hair a good, thorough once-over with it, sealing in all her hard work, which looked like vanilla icing on a cake.

A voice came over the intercom. "Josie, phone call. Josie, phone call."

"I have to take this. Be right back."

"But I need more spray! It's so hot out, my hair's gonna melt!"

Josie ran to the back room and got on the phone. It was her husband. Josie loved her husband. Crazy loved him. When he spoke she listened with every fiber of her being and could not get off the phone, especially when it concerned bad weather.

"If there is gonna be severe weather, I better wrap up and head out… now tell me again where the storm is?" Josie lit up another More cigarette. The smoke circled around her head like a halo.

She wheeled around with her orange, blazing cigarette, then POOF! Flames erupted.

Standing right in back of Josie was Madge—with her bangs on fire. She was lit up like sparklers on the Fourth of July.

"Jerry gotta go." Josie slammed the phone into the cradle.

"OOOOHHH DEAR! HELP! HELP!"

"Dear GOD in Heaven." Josie grabbed a half-full glass of iced tea and threw it on Madge's forehead, putting out the fire.

Madge sputtered and was simply beyond reason.

"OOOOH, GOD…you were trying to kill me!" Madge screamed as loud as a mama wildebeest whose young had just been eaten.

"Why did you walk into my cigarette?"

"Why did you turn around and put your butt in my hair? You ran off! I was trying to find you! I needed more hair spray!"

Josie rushed a wobbling Madge over to a shampoo chair.

"Madge, I am so sorry. Let me have a look at you." Josie grabbed her chin gently. "You have no burns on your face. Just a few singed locks. I'll fix you up right away."

"I have the Symphony Ball tonight. You have just ruined my hair. Hand me a mirror!"

Josie ran to her station and returned in a flash with a comb.

Trying to lighten the mood, Josie said, "I had a long-haired fluffy cat once that jumped up on the coffee table and walked over a candle and her fur went up in flames just like yours did. But she was just fine. The next minute she was outside chasing rats."

"Is that supposed to make me feel better?"

"I don't know, Madge," Josie said. "It was an accident. Here, let me fix the front."

Josie combed Madge's bangs, smoothing the burnt ends. "Perfect."

"Are you going to hand me a mirror?" said Madge. "DO YOU KNOW WHO I AM? I AM NOT TO BE TREATED LIKE THIS!"

"Here, take a look." Josie thrust a mirror in front of her face.

Madge examined her hairdo from every possible angle. "Well…I guess I'll make it."

Josie raised Madge's bangs and inspected her forehead. "Yep, just as ivory smooth as ever. You look like Miss America." Then she said. "Wait right there."

Josie ran into the back and emerged with a Polaroid camera.

"Smile, say cheese." Josie snapped a photo of Madge's amended hair helmet. "If there is any question when John gets back about how your hair looked, this will be my documented evidence that you look just as pretty as a picture."

Madge's car arrived, and Josie helped her into the long, black town car. When Madge was buckled up, Josie leaned in close to Madge's face.

"Madge, I am so sorry—from the depths of my heart and down to the tips of my toes. I was not trying to kill you," Josie said. "You do look real purty. Hope you enjoy your evening."

"Thank you, Josie," Madge said, with a half-smile. "We all do the best we can."

"Well, I gotta run. Heard a twister is headed this way." Josie shut the heavy door of the car. The engine gunned and coughed, and off Madge went to get ready for the Symphony Ball.

"Thank the Lord John will be back tomorrow." Josie pulled out another More cigarette from her smock pocket. "I don't think my heart can take another one of these episodes."

"Big Love"

The name, Victoria Gardens, sounded nice, like a pleasant place to smell flowers. Fragrant, not like death. Mom sat next to me in the passenger's seat, not asking for much, as was her sweet, sacred style. Her twiggy fingers, her sweet, pruney hands, once porcelain, had washed, cooked, loved, and lost. Now they patted her sweater as she sang.

Blue skies, smiling at me, nothing but blue skies, do I see.

In the rearview mirror, my childhood home hugged by a riot of weeds collapsed into a blur as we puttered away.

I sure would love some chocolate ice cream.

I brought you a gallon a few days ago.

It's all gone.

She plunged her wrists, oxblood and scarred from her attempts, into the blankety abyss of her fluffy skirt. If only she'd never found out about dad and Louise, his receptionist. If only my brother hadn't drowned.

My once-Amazonian mother had shrunk. Her hair boasted a runway of white roots hugged by Deep Raving Red. Her ancient, grey eyes were diamonds. Her beauty queen smile, front-tooth missing, my forever.

In 1966, the day I threw my Raggedy Ann out the window. I cried the minute it left my five-year-old mitts, the yarn hair clinging to my sticky palms. That evening, my tattered heart under my tear-stained gown was healed by her off-key lullaby and lilac scent.

Years later, she forgave me when I broke her mother's soup tureen. Then she housed me and my son after my life was shattered by divorce. She always picked up the pieces. Her love was Big.

Today was not the kind of thing that existed then. The future, a lie.

The pandemic had separated us. Her condition weakened, her sinews seemed to have dissolved into whispers.

The year had been a lifetime of phone calls. Confusing forms. Stacks of frenzied papers. Doctor visits. Finally, POA.

"We're going to your new apartment."

"Watch the curb," she lamented. "I love you."

The sun was shining and I hated it.

Under the porte cochère, at last. The quiet was stunning. I dialed. *Hello, we're here.* My hand, heavy like time, found her shoulder.

I opened her car door and cupped her sweet question-marked shaped body to my chest. We were one, once more. As I placed her crumbling frame into the cushioned wheelchair, I couldn't let her go.

Then like a guillotine, the cut came in one swift, benign push by a nameless human in grey scrubs, as she was wheeled away. Bald in back, her scalp a beautiful, bright moon.

I never want to do the right thing again.

THE END

Lisa Johnson Mitchell's work has appeared in *X-R-A-Y, Fictive Dream,* and *Cleaver,* among others. One of her pieces was a Finalist in the 2022 London Independent Story Prize Competition. Another received First Place in the 2021 *Button Eye Review* Summer Contest and placed in the Top 10 of the 2020 *Columbia Journal* Short Fiction Contest. Other works have been honored by *Glimmer Train*, ScreenCraft, and PEN Women. She was a resident at the Vermont Studio Center and holds an MFA from Bennington College.